Rebecca's Lost Journals

Also by Lisa Renee Jones

The Inside Out Series by Lisa Renee Jones

If I Were You

Being Me

Revealing Us

Rebecca's Lost Journals Vol. 1: The Seduction

Rebecca's Lost Journals Vol. 2: The Contract

Rebecca's Lost Journals Vol. 3: His Submissive

Rebecca's Lost Journals Vol. 4: My Master

The Master Undone: An Inside Out Novella

His Secrets

Rebecca's Lost Journals

Including the novella The Master Undone

Lisa Renee Jones

GALLERY BOOKS

New York   London   Toronto   Sydney   New Delhi

P
Jon

Gallery Books
A Division of Simon & Schuster, Inc.
1230 Avenue of the Americas
New York, NY 10020

8/1/14

Rebecca's Lost Journals, Volume 1: The Seduction copyright © 2013 by Lisa Renee Jones
Rebecca's Lost Journals, Volume 2: The Contract copyright © 2013 by Lisa Renee Jones
Rebecca's Lost Journals, Volume 3: His Submissive copyright © 2013 by Julie Patra Publishing, Inc.
Rebecca's Lost Journals, Volume 4: My Master copyright © 2013 by Julie Patra Publishing, Inc.
The Master Undone: An Inside Out Novella copyright © 2013 by Julie Patra Publishing, Inc.

These titles were previously published individually.

First Gallery Books bind-up edition April 2014

For information about special discounts for bulk purchases, please contact Simon & Schuster Special Sales at 1-866-506-1949 or business@simonandschuster.com.

The Simon & Schuster Speakers Bureau can bring authors to your live event. For more information or to book an event contact the Simon & Schuster Speakers Bureau at 1-866-248-3049 or visit our website at www.simonspeakers.com.

Manufactured in the United States of America

2   3   5   7   9   10   8   6   4   1

ISBN 978-1-4767-7210-3
ISBN 978-1-4767-7255-4 (ebook)

Contents

Rebecca's Lost Journals, Volume 1: The Seduction   1

Rebecca's Lost Journals, Volume 2: The Contract   39

Rebecca's Lost Journals, Volume 3: His Submissive   77

Rebecca's Lost Journals, Volume 4: My Master   125

The Master Undone: An Inside Out Novella   165

Excerpt from *If I Were You*   217

Rebecca's Lost Journals Vol. 1:
The Seduction

Journal 4, entry 1

Saturday, December 4, 2010

*H*ave you ever met someone who you immediately knew could change your life? I've heard about this happening, but I never experienced anything near it until tonight. Tonight I met him. I don't know this man's name, nor does he know mine, but I still feel the impact of our brief meeting deep inside.

I know where to find him again, but he doesn't know where to find me. I know how to figure out his name—but I won't. There are too many reasons why that would be a mistake. I can't allow myself to seek him out because he will, without question, lead me onto a path I know is better not taken. Already, I fear meeting him has stirred something inside me better left alone; something I crave, but know I do not dare indulge in. I can't imagine this man not leaving his mark on many women—and most men, as well.

He owns the air around him, and yours, too. He's strikingly male, strikingly attractive, exuding raw masculine power. He is what I think we all secretly want to be: in control of everything we are and everything we might one day be.

I'd do anything to know and understand who I truly am.

And I think that tonight, that was exactly what I was looking for: me. I just didn't realize it until I met him.

It started when I ended my shift at the bar and decided to go by the San Francisco Chocolate Factory and buy a box of chocolate to celebrate being alone. That sounds like a bitter pity party thing to write, but it's not. It's officially a year today since I buried my mother, and instead of letting grief consume me, I'm trying to be positive. (Something I haven't done a lot of since then.) So . . . the positive to this day is that I, Rebecca Mason, have survived, when I wasn't sure I would.

Somehow, though, instead of going straight to the chocolate store, I ended up two blocks away, standing outside the gallery I've dreamed of working at since way back when I started college five years ago. It just . . . happened. And at first it wasn't a good thing. One glimpse inside the gallery and the past year crashed down—burying my mother, deciding my art degree was worthless for paying the bills, learning things about my life I wish I never had. It was a little piece of hell standing there, hurting for what I have lost and what I can't have.

The worst part? I still crave my dream, to the point that I couldn't force myself to walk away without going inside the gallery. Not tonight, though I've spent a year away from that obsession. Not even the horrid waitress uniform beneath my long black leather coat could stop me from entering. I just buttoned up and went for it.

I walked inside, my bargain store heels clicking on the shiny expensive white tile, the soft sound of classical music playing in the background, and I was in heaven. I just stood there, staring at the sleek glass displays of art, and I sighed inside. This was where I still wanted to be, and why I went to school. It's been my love since I was a child, trying to create my own Picasso, only to realize I'm no artist myself. My gift is an eye for art, a deep love for it I can share with others. If only such things paid real money. How did I think I could be one of the few people who actually made a living in an art gallery?

But I did. There was a time when I thought I could. When I thought dreams were meant to be chased. That was before reality grabbed me by the throat and choked me into eye-opening revelations.

But standing there in that gallery tonight, I shoved all of that aside and just lost myself in the experience. I strolled from display to display, absorbing the gift of viewing the work of some of the most famous artists in the city and from around the world. I was enjoying myself until a salesperson, a blond and rather curvaceous woman, approached me with a snooty look that said she thought I was beneath the gallery. The bite of her attitude aroused my own fear that she was right, that I didn't belong there. But then the old me, the one who used to fight for what she wanted, reappeared out of nowhere. After a quick smoothing of my ruffled feathers, I asked her a few pointed questions about a certain artist's work to test her knowledge. She bristled and made an excuse to leave me alone. I'd almost forgotten I had this kind of cool composure inside me, and it felt amazing, rediscovering that part of myself.

I stayed for an hour, until they were about to close, and then I reluctantly headed to the front door. That was when he walked in, and I pretty much did the schoolgirl "weak in the knees" wilt I'd have sworn I was incapable of. But this man . . .

this man was impossibly overwhelming, and not just because he was sinfully good-looking. His eyes met mine and I froze, spellbound by his stare. I was aware of him in every cell of my being, in a way that I've never been aware of another man in my life.

I've been thinking about why that is. He was devastatingly handsome, but I've met gorgeous men before. It was more than his looks. It was definitely the edge of power and confidence he owned. The way he wore his perfectly fitted suit, rather than it wearing him. I keep telling myself his power and confidence was because he was a man, not a boy, at least a good ten years older than me. Surely that accounts for it—yet I can't imagine this man, even at twenty-two years old, not being what he is today.

Ultimately though, it wasn't his looks, his power, or even his mesmerizing eyes, which I thought maybe, just maybe, held a hint of male interest. It was the question he asked me: one that had enough impact to punch me in the chest and darn near level me. Such a simple question, from a man who was so not simple at all.

Did you come to apply for the internship?

I could barely process what he'd just said. I had to repeat the question in my head several times, and force calm thinking. And truthfully, I could have been insulted that he assumed my youth or something else about me meant I wasn't there to buy art. Instead, the elation of him considering me a prospect for a job at the gallery overrode any other reaction.

Then reality knocked out the ray of hope for my career. I know how an "internship" translates into dollars, because I'd done the math last year when my mother's funeral expenses had been a small fortune. Did I want to compete with a long list of people who would beg to work for pennies? Was I willing to work two jobs to survive? And really, how long could I do that? What was the real chance of making a full-time living at any gallery?

So what did I do? I laughed this silly, nervous laugh, and told him that working there was a dream I just couldn't afford. Then, before I did something even sillier, like change my mind, I stepped around him and left.

And now I eat my chocolate, sick to my stomach that I didn't find a reason to change my mind. Maybe if I eat the whole thing, I'll be too nauseated from sugar to feel sick about my decision. I can only hope.

Sunday, December 5, 2010

I went to bed thinking about the man from the gallery, and the way his silvery gray eyes had captured mine. About how I'd felt he would affect my life in some profound way when I'd met him. How would he do this if I never see him again? That was the last thing I remember thinking before I slipped into a dream.

No. A nightmare. In it, I'd been riding one of the trolleys, a cold San Francisco breeze whisking my long hair off my shoulders. Everything was vivid. The red car. The cold pole beneath my fingers. The shade of my light brown hair. The blue sky. The scent of the nearby ocean. Then suddenly my mother was there, riding with me, and she was smiling and happy in a way I haven't been since she died. I don't remember feeling happy in the dream, either. I remember feeling scared. And with good reason. A moment later, the trolley started to roll down a hill and it wouldn't stop. It was flying downward, faster and faster, and I was screaming, my heart in my throat. The trolley jumped the tracks and I clung to the pole, watching the water get closer and closer. Frantically, I searched for my mother, but she was just . . . gone. I was alone as the trolley slammed into the water.

The next thing I knew I was sitting up in bed, screaming bloody murder, my hand clutching my neck. I'm not sure how long it took me to calm down, but when I finally realized I was in my bed, in my apartment, I could smell my mother's vanilla and honey perfume, suffocating me, filling my nostrils and the entire bedroom. I swear, I felt my mother in my room.

She made me have that hellish nightmare. I'm aware that that sounds crazy and I'm not one who believes in ghost stories, but I know she did this. I just don't understand what it means. I thought she loved me—but then, I learned so much about her in her final days; things I sometimes wish I didn't know, but others I'm glad I do. It is only because of what I know now that I am willing to see what this nightmare might be telling me. Maybe I was always alone. Maybe that's why my mind placed my mother in my dream state and ripped her away.

Wednesday, December 8, 2010

Josh, the good-looking banker I went out with a couple times last month, came into the bar tonight asking why I hadn't returned his calls. How do you tell a guy that you dated him and had sex with him because you were lonely, and the net effect was still lonely? It wasn't that the sex was bad; it wasn't. I enjoyed it. I had an orgasm. I mean, that should account for something, because face it, how many first-time sexual encounters equal orgasm?

Well, maybe they do for some people, but not me. I tend to think too much the first time with a man. Not that I've had a lot of men in my bed. In fact, Josh is only the third. But I can just give myself an orgasm and it's much less complicated.

He's really a perfect guy—or he would be in my mother's book. Good-looking, self-made, loves his parents, and all that good stuff. He has money and appreciates everything he has, because he earned it himself. I just don't have it in me to play the relationship game right now. And maybe I can't appreciate or deserve someone like him until I know who I am.

I ended up telling him I was working crazy hours and I'd call him next week. I shouldn't have told him that. Why did I give him hope? I know how much hope can hurt.

Friday, December 10, 2010

I can't get the man from the gallery out of my mind, but I thought at least the nightmares had ended. Then I had the same hellish one last night, on the same trolley with my mother. I spent the morning and afternoon haunted by it, and for once I was thankful that Friday nights are so chaotic. That meant I'd be too busy to think about it or him.

But it's nearly ten o'clock, and I've barely had a break. I've been slammed with customers, yet that sick, horrible feeling when I'm plunging toward the water still suffocates me. It's frustrating and upsetting that I cannot get this nightmare out of my mind. It's affecting my job, and the tips I make to pay the bills.

I can't get rid of this sense that something is wrong, something bad is going to happen. I haven't felt like this since the week before my mother died. It's driving me crazy, and all I want to do is make this feeling go away. But I can't.

Monday, December 13, 2010

I dreamed of the man from the gallery, but remarkably I can't remember the details. I know it was dark and delicious, the way a man like that is meant to be dreamed about. Why can I remember the nightmare of being plunged into the bay by way of trolley car and my dead mother, yet the dream about a sexy, powerful man just plain escapes me? Truly, I don't know what is going on inside me right now, but I feel as if I am spinning out of control. It was enough to push me over the edge today, and I did what I said I wouldn't do: I found the man I had the encounter with at the gallery. I mean, what's the point in thinking that he's potentially life-changing if I avoid him?

His name is Mark Compton and he's the owner and manager of the gallery, and part of the family that owns Riptide, a famous auction house. That's who asked me if I was applying for a job. The owner. This feels like a sign, the reason he felt so important when I met him. Because he can hire me for the gallery and my dream job. And as crazy as this is for me to even think, let alone write down, I think he wanted me to apply for the internship. I think he wanted to hire me.

I want so badly to go apply now, even though it's probably too late. These jobs go so quickly and the competition would be fierce. To apply for the job and not get it would be devastating, yet I went so far as to see if I could get my hours cut at the bar to accommodate a second job. After all my years there, the new boss's answer was "no." The job market is tight and there are plenty of people willing to do my job without special scheduling. So unless I can find a more flexible second job, I couldn't even take the internship anyway.

This is insanity. I can't do it. I just can't. Damn Mark Compton for tempting me and making me think that maybe, just maybe, I can chase this dream again.

Wednesday, December 15, 2010

*T*his time the nightmare was worse. This time I hit the water, the icy cold ocean claiming me as I was submerged, struggling to stop the trolley from crushing me. The splintering pain of drawing water into my lungs and trying to get to the surface. Pushing to the top with all my might to find my mother there, shoving me back down. I am angry, more angry than I've been in a long time—and I've been plenty angry. Angry at her for leaving me. Angry at her for lying to me. Angry at her for shoving me back into the water, and . . . and what? What the hell does this nightmare mean? This feeling of dread, of death, just won't go away.

I have to go to work and perform a job I hate. Maybe I just won't go. But damn it, I have to go. How else will I survive?

Friday, December 17, 2010

I've tried not to think about this being my first Christmas alone. I've tried to block out the trees, songs, and holiday cheer I used to embrace. It hasn't worked. Next up, New Year's resolutions. I've never made resolutions. I mean—why? Who really keeps them?

But I am thinking about next year, and my life in general. If life is short, why live it waiting tables at a bar? It's all I can think of today. How did I become the one in my group of college friends who has done nothing with my life, when I was the only one who knew what I wanted to do with my life? Now all my friends have moved on to new things. Casey is married to a banker and barely has time for me. Darla's in New York working for a television station. Susan is in Seattle working for a PR firm. Okay, there is Kirk, who still works at the Burger Palace and has absolutely no motivation to do anything different. Like me.

How have I become this? How have I let my dreams slip away? I have to do something. I have to fix this. I have to fix me. Being inside that gallery made me the happiest I have been in too long to remember.

Christmas Eve Morning

I'm working at the bar tonight, a glad volunteer. Just call me the Grinch, because I'd rather skip Christmas this year. I haven't had the nightmare again, though I still have that vague sense of foreboding I can't get rid of. After careful thought, I think the death that I sense and fear is the death of my art dreams.

So I've been thinking. What makes one person's dreams come true when another's don't? Determination. Action. Desire. Those are the things I once embraced, and I chose to do that again when I woke up this morning. I walked to the gallery's neighborhood and went inside every fancy restaurant that pays big tips, and managed to score a job at a place right by the gallery. I then called the gallery and asked if the internship was still open, and it wasn't. It was a hard answer to hear, but I was told I could still put in an application for the future. I did and wistfully wished Mark Compton was there. My gut tells me that seeing him again is my ticket to getting a job.

Now that I've decided to do this, maybe I can take an unpaid internship in hopes of proving myself. I'll hang on to this new waitressing job and stop by the gallery once a week until I get a job there, paid or unpaid. I have to be brave enough to take risks. Besides, the new job pays better than my old one. This is a good move. I have to believe that.

Saturday, December 25, 2010

*M*ovies alone. A huge tub of popcorn. A box of chocolate. A large soda. Stomachache. A stupid movie choice that made me cry like a baby in the theater and wish I'd brought my makeup to fix my face. Calls with friends. I told them I was with a hot guy I met at the bar. Bedtime. New job starts tomorrow.

Monday, December 27, 2010

I was breathless when Mark sauntered into the restaurant, owning the place—tall, blond, and deliciously male in a custom-fitted gray suit—and turning heads, both male and female. Not many men make me breathless, but there aren't many men who can claim the very air that exists around them, as he does.

Kim, the sweet hostess from Tennessee who I'm fast becoming friends with, seated him in my section, and I was ridiculously nervous as I headed to his table to take his order. I didn't expect him to remember me. Okay, maybe I did. Or at least I hoped he would. I wanted to be right about what had passed between us. I wanted him to have wanted me to apply for the internship. I wanted him to ask me about it again now, and spare me walking into the gallery later and asking myself—especially after waiting on his table.

So I approached him, and the minute I stepped to his table, he arched a brow at me and asked how I could afford to work at the restaurant but not for him. I surprised myself by not missing a beat, but I've always been good under pressure with professors and even the artists whom I encountered through my studies, no matter how arrogant or sharp-witted. And Mark is arrogant. Oh, yes. It radiates off him, and somehow it's sexy on him when it would be pompous on someone else. So it went something like this.

"I know how little internships pay," I replied.

"How can you know how much my internship pays if you didn't apply?"

"I know the industry."

"How?"

"I went to school to be in it, which I'm sure you assumed or you wouldn't be asking me this."

His lips did this sexy, amused kind of half smirk. Oh, the mouth on that man. "Why don't you apply and find out?"

"I already did."

"Even though you can't afford the dream of working there?"

"I had a moment of weakness."

We stared at each other, and I got warm all over in a way I've never felt with a man. Not good with a potential boss, I know, but it happened. Slowly, his gaze lowered and he glanced at my name tag, and he might as well have been licking my nipples. I have no idea what happened. I had to squeeze my thighs together.

He returned his gaze to mine and softly said my name. Just "Rebecca," but it was all soft and rough at the same time, and I melted into a big puddle right there in front of him. The look on his face was pure satisfaction, as if he knew what he'd just done and he reveled in it.

And so did I, because this is what a woman wants a man to be able to do to her. The feeling of him controlling my pleasure so easily was just mind blowing. I'd never experienced something so intense before, let alone in a public place.

The erotic, exquisite moment ended abruptly when a gorgeous brunette in a pencil skirt and low-cut red silk blouse walked up to the table and gave me a look that could have singed me. I was suddenly very aware of my hair pulled into a bun, and the simple light blue skirt and white blouse provided by the restaurant.

How had I thought for one moment this man wanted me, when he has a woman like this? But you know, after my initial embarrassment, it was almost a relief to know that his interest in me was business. I could take a job with Mark if it came about, and not worry about a conflict of interest between my hormones and my job performance.

And not an hour after Mark left the restaurant, I got a call for a job interview at the gallery. Not with Mark, but with someone by the name of Ralph, but who cares? It's tomorrow and I got the impression it was almost a technicality. I assume that means they checked my references and I made an impression on Mark.

That probably means I'm working for pennies, but I've decided to go for it. I have a good feeling about this. This is the first time in weeks I don't have that feeling of foreboding. So I must have been mourning the career I thought I'd never have.

Tuesday, December 28, 2010

*H*ired!

I got the job at the gallery, and the pay is better than I expected. Just a little, but every bit counts. There was a lot that was unexpected about this day, like how the interview played out. Ralph turned out to be this funny and charming Asian man. He took me to the break room and we sat and had coffee, which he seems to live on. The man is a hyper chit-chatter who loaded me up on staff gossip. Of course, he warned me that Mark—Mr. Compton to the staff—was tough as nails, but fair.

He made me laugh and put me at ease and was encouraging in every way. We were laughing, and I had let my guard down, when Mark walked into the room. I swear, it was like the room's temperature rose ten degrees. Okay, I rose ten degrees, but looking at Ralph, I'm pretty sure he did, too. I'm pretty sure he's gay (not many straight men wear pink bow ties, and it suited Ralph quite nicely), so we are of like mind where Mark is concerned. Mark is the definition of the word MAN.

As Mark filled his coffee cup, Ralph and I just sat there and soaked in the raw sexual power he oozed. After he was done, Mark leaned on the counter and fixed me with one of those intense gray stares I don't know if I'll ever get used to. Then he asked who my favorite artists are. I told him my favorite was always the one I have yet to discover. He just stared at me, and I have no idea if he liked the answer or not. But he clearly wasn't satisfied that I knew my art, because the drilling began. He asked who was my favorite artist I'd already discovered in a number of genres, and then argued with me about why one of my choices wasn't a good one. My nerves slid away. Art has a way of making the world slip away for me.

"That's a rather shortsighted opinion," he'd said dryly, "when there are artists in the genre who have achieved so much more."

"That's where I'd say you're being shortsighted," I'd replied. Ralph choked on his coffee; I'm guessing not too many people argue with Mark. I went on to explain how the artist I'd named had yet to show the world all he had to offer, while the more well-known ones he'd named had already reached their peaks.

Mark looked amused at that answer and maybe a little surprised. I'm not sure. Reading that man is pretty impossible. We went on to debate several artists he named and then just like that, he pushed off the counter and said, "You start tomorrow, Ms. Mason."

And then he just left.

Wednesday, December 29, 2010

I worked both jobs today and I don't know how I have the energy to write this, but my head is spinning and I can't possibly sleep. I like the restaurant so much more than the bar, and I made double the tips that I'm used to in one night. That's wonderful and all, but it's the gallery I am in love with, the place I yearn to make my life.

Today was sensory overload, with the art I adore and my man-candy boss. He's arrogant and demanding, and he intimidates everyone but me. I can't explain it, but I feel challenged and excited around him, not like a wilting little flower. But then, I've never been a wilting flower. I guess being raised by a single mother who was tough as nails helped, even if she was as bitter as lemons at times about the father who deserted us. Of course, that was a lie, but I'm not ruining today by going down that path.

Back to Mark . . . Mr. Compton, that is. I think it's kind of sexy, the way he calls me Ms. Mason, though I wonder why he calls the front desk intern, Amanda, by her first name. How many times did he say Ms. Mason today and send a shiver straight down my spine?

"Good morning, Ms. Mason."

"This is your office, Ms. Mason."

"Ms. Mason, you have homework and there will be testing. You must be cultured and able to talk about anything and everything your customer base might find of interest."

And to that one I had thought, Oh, please, yes. Test me. Hey, a girl can fantasize. It's almost safer when you know the man has some ridiculously sexy woman in his life, so it's just innocent dreaming.

And finally, the point I'm getting to, the big-one whopper he threw me that sent my pulse into overdrive. "Ms. Mason, I expect you to attend a party at Ricco Alvarez's house with me tomorrow night."

Ricco Alvarez, as in the fabulous, talented, and famous artist. I can't believe I'm not only going to his party, but I'm going with Mark! It's business, I know, but the funny thing is that this sixth sense told me not to mention the party to the rest of the staff. Instead, I discreetly asked around and no one else is going to the party. Not even Mary, the sales rep I had the issue with the first night I visited the gallery. She and I are not off to a grand start as it is. Mentioning the party might have been the last straw for our working relationship.

So, hmmm . . . why isn't Mary invited to the party? Maybe she's on her way out the door and that's why Mark hired me? But why not tell me to keep the party hush-hush if he wants to replace her? Then again, I can't see Mark caring if Mary feels nervous or upset over what he does. He seems to box business into business with nothing personal involved. I'm an investment to Mark, I think. I can't explain why, but it's another gut feeling I have. Mary might have once been, too, but not now. He seems to almost ignore her. I feel kind of sad for her. Though I want the job, there's no appeal in hurting someone else to get to the top. It kind of makes the idea of worrying about having nothing to wear to the party seem shallow, when her job could be on the line.

Saturday, January 1, 2011

I don't even know where to begin this entry, and I only have an hour to get to work at the restaurant. I just know that I don't want to forget any details and I need to write them when I'm fresh. I'm certain I'll look back at this at some point and crave the feelings and memories as clearly as they were in my mind tonight.

To start, Mark had me change clothes and then meet him at the gallery before the party. The entire staff knew I was attending the party with him and Mary was just plain mean. She popped into my office and said, "I guess it takes the right skirt to climb the ladder around here." I assume she was calling me a slut; her tone said she was. It wasn't easy to remind myself she was probably feeling threatened and bite my tongue, but I did.

Mark and I rode to the party in his Jaguar. I don't even HAVE a car, so it was a luxurious ride for me, for sure. And being in that car alone with him was impossibly intimate. I swear, when I am with him, I feel him in every part of me. I think he feels it, too. Or maybe not. But even if there is an attraction between us, it can't work out. He's my boss and he has another woman.

Ricco's home is in a ritzy area of the city and it's elegant in every possible way. And Ricco himself is not only fabulously talented, he's striking in person. Not beautiful like Mark, but there's something about the way his sharp features and deep-set eyes come together. Very arrogant and regal, almost hard. But I also sensed a softer part of him that I think is part of his creativity. I really bonded with Ricco and he stayed by my side most of the night; he even invited me to have coffee with him next week. I thought Mark would be pleased, but for some reason he wasn't. He kept watching me with Ricco, and more than once, he appeared in the middle of our conversation and just listened. Maybe he was evaluating how I handle clients. I can't be sure.

Despite Mark's irritation with me, when the night was over he offered to drive me home. He walked me to my door and I swear he wanted . . . something. Not a kiss. It's not that simple with Mark. Maybe he wanted to fuck me, but I didn't let my mind go there. I just stood there, trying to figure out what it was he wanted.

What was it that I wanted? The only word that comes to mind is "more" for me. For him, I had this uneasy moment of thinking "too much." Mark would want too much, and somehow it would never be enough. I have no idea why I feel this, but I do. It's insanity for my mind to be in this place anyway. He's my boss. He might be able to separate whatever that "too much" is, but could I? Would I end up ruining my dream for mere hot sex, over and done with?

Yes. I'm beginning to think that is where this could go, and I won't let it. Or maybe I'm imagining the whole thing. Mark still calls me Ms. Mason and I call him Mr. Compton. He hasn't touched me. He hasn't made one remark that is even remotely sexual. I have no reason to believe we are headed toward naked and starving for each other, unless it's in my dreams. And that is one dream that I'm confident I could recall in vivid detail . . .

Sunday, January 2, 2011

*T*oday I had coffee with Ricco at the coffee shop next door to the gallery. I was shocked when I arrived early to discover that the gorgeous brunette I'd seen with Mark at the restaurant is Ava, the woman who owns the place. Not only that, she wasn't rude or snotty at all this time. She's probably closer to Mark's age than mine, and carries herself almost regally, maybe too much so—like it's a way to hide what she doesn't want seen. She seemed to want to build a friendship, but I couldn't quite feel right about it with the conflicting impressions I've had of her. She laughed and joked with me, and asked me how I was handling Mark being so controlling. I wondered if she was trying to get me to say something she'd then repeat to Mark. That's so cynical of me, but it's what popped into my head and I never say anything I don't want repeated. She even whispered a warning about how temperamental Ricco can be. (But I'd heard the same from Ralph and Amanda.)

She did enough talking for both of us, and it turns out she's known Mark and Ricco for years and they are all friends, though I'm not sure how this many gorgeous people are ever just friends. Some people would say that is small-minded of me, but it is what it is. I was surprised that I liked Ava. I'm not sure what to make of her. I'm going to be cautious with her, that's for sure.

I didn't say much about Mark or Ricco to her. I don't even share things with the people I know well. There were too many years of my mother working double shifts at the hotel she managed, warning me not to talk to strangers while she was gone. Not to tell people whom I knew things that they could let slip to someone else, who would know I was alone. She was so crazily insistent that I learned to write stuff down. It's better that way, I've found. I'm the only one judging me or influencing my own thoughts. I think most people let others decide who and what they are too much.

As for Ricco, he was amazing to me, and I saw nothing that screamed of his reputation for being temperamental. I warmed to him immediately, just as I had at his party. He's one of the few people I've ever felt this comfortable with this quickly. He has this protective vibe about him that I found surprisingly appealing. Maybe it's because he's a good fifteen years older than me and almost fatherly, though he's far too sexy a man for me to ever think of that way, and I feel no deep, burning need for a father figure. I don't need or want to be taken care of. He tugs on some deep part of me, though. Really, he and Mark both do, but for different reasons. With Mark, I think it's all about raw power and just plain lust. With Ricco, maybe there's friendship? I just don't know.

We were about to leave when I saw Ava talking to a man at the counter dressed in Harley boots, jeans, and a leather jacket.

The look on her face said she was in lust. I sure hope I'm not that obvious when I look at Mark. Then the man turned around and I took in the sweeping whole picture he made, including collar-length mussed-up blond hair that screamed "wild and wicked rock star delicious," and I could see why she was looking at him that way. Ricco followed my attention, and the two men waved at each other.

Then the next thing I knew, I was meeting the "rock star," who was the incredibly famous Chris Merit. The man's art sells for scary, wonderfully big price tags. As for the wild part I'd assumed, he didn't come off that way. He was all business, about to head to a meeting with Mark, and Chris wanted to confirm that Ricco was still donating a painting to the next Riptide auction for a children's cancer charity he supports. Despite the two being cordial, I didn't get the impression Chris and Ricco were all that fond of each other. I think Ricco has a problem connecting with most people, but I think he's just artistic and misunderstood. I'm going to his private studio this weekend to preview the work he's willing to let me show to special customers, and I'm beyond thrilled.

I returned to the gallery and was called into Mark's office. The power that man oozes from behind his desk is enough to make me forget every other man and my name. He then proceeded to drill me about Ricco and to warn me that artists could use my eagerness for success to manipulate me. He said it was his responsibility to protect me. I told him I didn't need protection. His reply: My gallery. My employee. My protection. Those words were laced with possessiveness, and the way he'd looked at me . . . I felt more naked than I have felt with my legs spread wide for any other man. The air thickened with awareness between us. And then, in a snap, it was gone as if it had never happened, and maybe it didn't. Maybe it was my imagination.

Mark proceeded to test me on the material he'd given me to study. I'm pleased that I passed with flying colors despite my crazy work schedule. I'm not as pleased about being tested every afternoon in his office, but that's his plan. Until I convince him I'm ready, Mark won't put me on the showroom floor. He was quick to tell me that he plans to push me to my limits.

I left the meeting with the same feeling I'd had the night I'd visited the gallery the first time. This man is going to have a profound impact on my life.

Friday, January 7, 2011

*H*ot banker dude Josh showed up at my door right after I got home tonight. This is what happens when you are a chicken and don't return phone calls. He had a bottle of wine and roses for me. I tried to be strong. I told him I wasn't in a place to date. He said okay, let's just share the wine.

I should have said no again. But he just looked so scrumptious and smelled so good, and I felt bad about not calling him back. The next thing I knew, I was naked and he was licking me all over and I was panting like a wanton wench who didn't have any sense in her head. I blame Mark for turning me wet and wanting every time he walks into the room. And I already knew Josh was gifted with his tongue, and boy was he. I was quivering with release in no time.

I tried to repay the orgasm by giving him a blow job, but

he didn't let me. He decided to lick me all over again and gave me yet another orgasm. The man was determined to win me over. Then he fucked me and he did it well. That man hit all the right spots in all the right ways.

I should have been won over. So why was it still not enough? I know he thought it would be; I saw it in his eyes. I told him nothing had changed, and he said okay again, we'd be fuck buddies. If he'd meant it, I might think it wasn't such a bad idea. A no-commitment kind of thing. I don't have time for more than a wham-bam-hit-me-with-an-orgasm-or-two kind of relationship.

Only, he didn't mean it. This gorgeous man with bedroom skills very few men possess, who is sweet and sexy, and successful, must have a long list of woman chasing him, but he wants me. I told him I didn't think the fuck buddy thing would work out. He told me he'd show up with another bottle of wine and convince me otherwise.

Oh, yes. I made a mistake by fucking him last night. I've opened up a big can of trouble.

Saturday, January 8, 2011

I visited Ricco's home today and took a tour of his private gallery. It was spectacular and he had a Mexican chef prepare an authentic Mexican meal for us that was amazing. I asked him millions of questions about his art and his creative process and he answered them all. And when he asked me about my life, I shocked myself by almost crying when I told him about my mother dying of lung cancer. I don't know why I told him, and I absolutely don't know why I almost cried. And now, why can't I stop thinking of the nightmare I haven't had in weeks, where my mother pushed me back under the water of the bay?

Monday, January 10, 2011

*M*ark informed me that my first time working with actual customers would be at a gallery event Wednesday afternoon that will carry into early evening. I'm thrilled, but I have to work at the restaurant that night and I can't get the time off. I tried. So it's going to be this nightmare of a challenge to do well at the gallery and then rush to the restaurant.

Monday, January 17, 2011

*T*onight there was a wine tasting at the gallery and I had to work at the restaurant right after the event, just like last week. I made it to work last week, so I was sure I could do so again this week. Working two jobs has been killing me, but ever since Mark let me loose on the sales floor I've done well.

The event this evening seemed to be going well, too. I made an expensive sale and landed a number of contacts I know will equal more sales. I was feeling good until the event ran late, and Mary had some crisis to deal with, and Mark asked me to stay. But I couldn't, without losing my job at the restaurant. The instant I told him this, Mark called me into his office. He shut the door and I leaned against it. He was close, his gray eyes glinting with irritation.

"You work for me or you work for them. Choose now, Ms. Mason."

"It's not about choice, Mr. Compton. It's about the neces-
sity of paying my bills."

"You'll never turn this job into a larger income if you can't
complete duties."

Since when was this an option? I rebutted, "I haven't been
told I have any chance to make more money."

"You just started."

"My bills didn't."

That glint in his eyes had turned sharper and I was sure he
was going to fire me. Instead, he'd said, "Ten percent on tonight's
sale to get you by. If you continue to do well, there will be more.
But that's on the condition that you quit the restaurant. It's beneath you, and I don't share unless it's on my terms. This isn't."

I had barely been able to breathe. He'd just offered me a huge
bonus and given me the chance to make this job my career and
actually get paid for it? I'm not going to get my hopes up. Not yet.

Thursday, February 3, 2011

So much has changed in the past two weeks. To Mark's dis-
pleasure, I gave a short notice at the restaurant. It was so crazy
busy, juggling both jobs, that I didn't have time to write in my
journals. I still haven't, despite leaving the restaurant fully a
week ago. There have been events at the gallery, and . . . there
has been another big change. Him.

He's become a huge part of my life. He, who wants to be
known simply as "Master," has swept into my world and torn
away walls I never knew existed, and that I'm not sure I want
torn down. But he wants to tear them down. He says he will

control me, command my body, and show me pleasure like I've never known. He will show me trust that is the greatest bond two people can share. He will fuck me senseless, and then do it again and again until I know nothing but him.

Why does this appeal to me? Why am I considering this? If I know nothing but him, where will I be? How will I exist? He hasn't touched me yet, but I feel as if he has. Josh showed up with wine, and nothing he could do could entice me this time. There is only him, my would-be "Master." And that is what he wants. I share my joys and fears and pain with him. He will show me rewards and escapes.

When he first told me I was a natural submissive, I didn't believe him. I lean on no one. But he says that makes me need the outlet he can offer: the place where I can safely hand over all that I am, and just feel. It frightens me to realize how much this idea seeps into me and flows so easily. Handing over control to this man terrifies me . . . but it also arouses me like nothing in this lifetime ever has, besides art.

He wants to meet tomorrow night, to give me a small taste of what he is offering me. He promises to start slow and give me the chance to test the waters before we go very far, and before we sign an agreement as a true Master and Submissive.

An agreement that says he owns my body.

Friday, February 4, 2011

My first submissive experience is tonight. I still can't believe I'm doing this. I still can't believe I want this. How has two weeks changed so much about what I know of myself? The woman who wants this isn't me, and yet she is. Or maybe it's because of who he is? Had any other man presented this to me, I would have laughed. He's sunk deep into my body and soul and stirred something molten and thick with possibilities outside my realm of full understanding.

He's invited me to his home and will send a car to pick me up, because he said as "his" (like he owns me), I wouldn't be taking trolleys to the places I needed to go. My objection was waved away and he made himself clear: When I am his, I will be taken care of. There was no "if" to his statement. His desire to own me scares me more than the unknowns of a BDSM relationship. I've only depended on one person in my life, my mother, who not only died, but betrayed me in ways that still cut deep.

The choice to get into the car and come to him was mine, he'd said. I had to make the decision, knowing what waited for me. Knowing the instant I crossed the entryway, I was under his control.

Sunday, February 6, 2011

*L*ast night was amazing. When the car came, I was taken to a spa instead of his house. I had my hair and makeup done, plus a full wax. He even had a dress there waiting for me. Red, short, clingy. No panties or bra allowed underneath, per his note in the box. Also per the note, the driver would give me the choice when I returned to the car to either go home to my apartment or go to him. There was no question in my mind: I was going to him.

I remember settling into the comfort of the soft leather seat and how shockingly aroused I was, just imagining what my submissive experience might be like. My thighs had been slick, my nipples tight and tingling. It really was an insane reaction when I hadn't even made it to his home yet.

Once I was there, my adventure truly began. He opened the door and his presence slid over me, wickedly hot and powerful, washing away the coldness of the night. He wore soft faded jeans and a T-shirt. His feet were bare, as if he was ready to be naked in a flash. I wanted him to be naked in that moment. I think I always want him to be naked.

He motioned me inside and I stepped over the entryway. He shut the door behind me, but didn't touch me. Instead he stepped in front of me again, and his gaze swept my scantily clad body, lingering on my tightly puckered nipples, male appreciation glowing from the depths of his gaze.

When his eyes lifted to mine again, he said, "Last chance to back out."

I lifted my chin and met his stare. "I don't want to back out."

Satisfaction slid over his face. "Then there are rules."

"Rules?" My knees were liquid, my body one big, eager nerve ending. I wanted his rules. I can't explain why. I don't understand why.

"Rules," he confirmed. "To start, you don't speak unless I ask a question. You don't do anything I don't tell you to do. You do exactly what I say you do. Normally, I would say I'll also do anything I wish to you, but until we have an agreement with your limits, I'll refrain from going places I might otherwise go."

Some part of me rebelled. This isn't me. I don't get commanded by anyone but myself. But it was me.

"Understand?" he asked.

"Yes." I couldn't keep the tremble from my voice.

"If at any point you want to stop, say 'Stop,' but mean it if you say it. If you tell me to stop, I will. 'Stop' tells me you are at your limit. Or you can choose another word."

I nodded. I did want another word. "I think . . . I might say stop by accident."

"Then choose a word."

I hadn't had a clue what to choose, and he seemed to sense that because he said, "Red. That's your safe word until you choose another. Say it and I stop."

"Yes."

He'd studied me so long and so intently that it was all I could do not to scream at him to speak. And finally he did. "Get on your knees."

I blinked at him, a bit taken aback, but I did as he ordered.

"Unzip my pants and suck me."

Looking back now, this command should have bothered me. Shouldn't it have? Being ordered to my knees to serve him? But it didn't. In fact, it was enticing. It made me feel in control. I'd take his pleasure. I'd own him while he was trying to own me.

I stroked the thick ridge of his erection, and tugged down his zipper before finding his hard, hot flesh with my palm and freeing his cock. I stroked him slowly and liquid formed on the tip of his erection.

"Lick it off," he ordered.

I looked up at him, watching him as my tongue snaked out and lapped at the pre-cum, shocked when he'd showed no reaction at all, since I'd been determined to get one. I wrapped my hand around the width of him and began to lick and suck. I expected his hand to go to my head, but it didn't. This drove me nuts.

"Harder," he ordered. "Faster."

I complied, more determined than ever to get the reaction from him I wanted. And finally his hand was in my hair, his hips pumping against me, his cock sliding up and down my throat.

But I had been the one out of control, not him. I had nearly orgasmed from doing that to him; I'd been so damn aroused by the idea of making him release. And when he finally did, oh, man, he growled in this gravelly sexy way, deep in his throat, and I don't know how I didn't come as well.

The next thing I knew, he pulled me to my feet and pushed me against the door, facing it, so my hands were on the hard surface. Then he yanked my dress over my head, exposing me to his view, his touch. I stood there in my high heels and nothing else, and he leaned into me, touching me from calf to back, and it was a blessed relief to feel him close. His hands were all over me, stroking my breasts, pinching my nipples, roaming over my backside. His fingers pressed into the swollen wetness between my thighs and that was all it took. I orgasmed.

He turned me to face him again. "Follow me," he ordered. He turned and started walking. I followed him like his slave, and I know that is what he intended. Master. Slave. He owned me then, but would he in the future?

We ended up in a large bedroom with a massive bed in the center and cabinets on the walls that I guessed held erotic toys that would terrify and thrill me. I was right. He ordered me to stand by the bed, and then opened a drawer and pulled out some sort of band with two arm cuffs on either end.

Adrenaline poured through me at the idea of being tied up, but I didn't feel scared. I felt like I was on fire, burning alive with the need to have this man inside me. When he ordered me to raise my hands I did. Before I knew it, I was in the center of the bed, my hands attached to the headboard above me, and he was naked and straddling me with some sort of crop in his hand. A momentary fear overcame me until he promised me he was only going to let me get a feel for what the leather felt like this time. No pain. Only pleasure.

And it was pleasure. The snap and pressure against my nipples, my clit, even my legs and arms, was shockingly exquisite. The things he did to me . . . I can't even write some of them down. I was bothered, though, by how he hadn't kissed me, uncertain what that meant. What this relationship really was. How it seemed to demand so much in some ways and offer so little in others.

But it's the things that happened this morning that affected me more than last night. I don't remember falling asleep. I just remember the nightmare and waking up. I'd been back on the trolley, the air a cold arctic blast around me. So very cold that my lips were purple and my teeth chattered. My mother wasn't there. No one was there.

The car began to go faster and faster into this eternal black hole, and I could see nothing but darkness. The splash of icy water came in a blast and pain splintered through me. I pushed away from the steel machine that threatened to take me under and my mother was in the water above me, but she wasn't alone.

There was someone else there. Someone she was fighting with. They blocked my way to the surface and I tried to swim around them, but something grabbed my legs and sucked me deeper.

I sat up in the bed screaming bloody murder and he was there, holding me, telling me I was safe, that he was there for me. The hard man who'd ordered me to suck him and fuck him was now gentle and caring, a total contrast to the night before. I've never in my life felt safe because of anyone except my mother, but I felt safe in his arms. I felt right there. And it terrified me almost as much as the nightmare.

I can't be with him. I can't need someone else as much as I think I will come to need him. I just . . . can't. I haven't told him. He didn't ask. I'm not sure why. Because he changed his mind? Because he didn't like what he thought my answer would be? And if I don't want to enter into this agreement with him, why do I care?

Monday, February 7, 2011

*T*he day that started out with me fretting over my would-be "Master" was made better when I got a call from a local retiree I'd been trying to buy a painting from. He was willing to sell. Mark was beyond impressed when I told him I had landed a Georgia O'Nay for the Riptide auction. We drove out together to pick it up, and my day ended with a promotion, thanks to the small fortune Riptide will make when the painting sells.

I am now in charge of all Riptide auctions for the gallery, and Mary will now go through me for approval. I will get 10 percent of every sale I organize. She wasn't happy. I'm ecstatic. My life is

changing. I don't need someone's protection. I don't need someone to control me. So why does the absence of any attempt at an
agreement send me to bed tonight feeling so very alone?

Monday, February 14, 2011

Once again it's Valentine's Day.

Josh and Ricco both sent me roses. Ricco attached a nice
note about celebrating my new career. Josh signed his "your
friendly fuck buddy." I cringed. Mark didn't give me anything.
He was just Mark, forever sexy and enthralling, and judgmen-
tal, and too many other things to list. Mary gave me the cold
shoulder. Ralph stole two roses from me for his desk. I worked
late and locked up the gallery. When I exited, a car was waiting for me. To my surprise when I got inside, he was there. He
fucked me right there, in front of the gallery, with the driver
inside. I let the man in the front seat watch. I let him hear me
moan. I just . . . did. I don't even talk about my sex life, but I let
a stranger watch me fuck another man.

And when it was over and I was delivered to my door, my
"Master" handed me a package that is now sitting in front of
me on my bed. Inside, I found a contract. I'd be submissive to
my "Master." He'd control me. There is a long list of things
he'd expect of me. The note inside promised that we'd negotiate details, but it also said that I have to instigate the next
meeting, so that he knows I really want this. And when I do,
I should wear the gift included in my package. It's a gorgeous
rose-shaped gold ring I found nestled in a velvet box. The
note attached to it read, "Wearing it means you belong to me."

I don't know what to do. I don't know how I feel, and I have no one to talk to. Even if I did, how do I talk to someone about this? I've sat here doing internet searches on BDSM relationships, but I've done this many times before.

Now, I'm sitting here listening to the Dr. Kat Sex Talk show as callers ask her questions about sex and relationships, and I am actually tempted to call. But I can't. I don't talk to people about my private life. And I sure don't talk on public radio.

Wednesday, February 16, 2011

Silence. The ball is in my court. He really does seem to expect me to go to him now and pursue the contract. I am still confused and uncertain about what I want. I'm sitting on my bed, listening to Dr. Kat again, and I like her. She is fun and honest, and makes sense when she responds to people. I am almost desperate enough to dial the number provided, and use an alias, though I expect the callers are lined up long in advance. But maybe I'll try . . .

Yes. I think I'll try.

"Welcome to the Dr. Kat show. What's your question?"

"A man has asked me to enter into a BDSM relationship with him and this is new to me," I told her. "I'm not sure how to be certain that it's right for me."

"Is this your first BDSM experience?"

"Yes. Yes, it is."

"Well then, it's normal to feel uncertain. Will you be bottom or top?"

"Bottom or top?"

"Are you the submissive?"

"Yes."

"And how do you feel about that?"

My reply was speedy. "I've never thought of myself as submissive, but he says I need an outlet where I don't have to be in control."

"Do you?"

"I didn't, but now . . . maybe."

"What's your hesitation? Is he pressuring you to do things you aren't comfortable with?"

"No. He's given me space and time to make this decision."

"That's good," Dr. Kat said with approval. "That's how it should be, but you're still hesitating. Why?"

"I'm afraid of losing who I am, and being only what he lets me be."

"It sounds like you're afraid of losing control. For many people, giving away control in a safe BDSM environment can actually help them get over this fear. It sounds like you're drawn to the idea."

"Yes . . . yes, I think I am, but I'm nervous."

"The important thing is to set limits, the things you won't tolerate. Talk to him, and if he won't agree to those limits, then you need to consider if this is right for you. He only has control because you give it to him. Don't ever forget that."

I hung up from my call with Dr. Kat and sat there thinking about limits and control. I never thought I'd see the day I would give a man any control over me at all. Now, my biggest fear is giving one too much.

Rebecca's Lost Journals Vol. 2: The Contract

Journal 5, entry 1

Thursday, February 17, 2011

*M*aster. Submission. A contract that says he *owns* me for his personal pleasure. It's my decision whether to dare to tread that path or not. Sitting here on my bed in fluffy pajamas with a glass of wine in hand, these things seem like they are meant for someone else's life, not mine.

Truly, I'm surprised that this decision wasn't the only thing on my mind at work today. I was certain that it, and the man involved, even the call to Dr. Kat, would consume me all day. But art is a gift to this world that I'm passionate about, and its allure enticed me away from my fretful worries about handing over control to a man I barely know but find impossible to resist. Being able to separate him from my art is actually quite comforting. I don't have to lose who I am to be a part of who he is.

By midmorning I wasn't even thinking about the contract points I wanted to discuss with him, or of having been tied to his bed. Or all the wicked things he'd done to me while I was tied there, or even all the wicked things he might do to me in the future. A customer gave me a tip about a man in Seattle who had a rare masterpiece he was thinking of letting go for a steal.

It took me hours to track him down, but I actually managed to get through to him. I talked him into meeting with Mark about auctioning it off through Riptide. Mark was in NYC at Riptide today, so I had to call him. I'm smiling just replaying the way the call went. I do enjoy verbally sparring with my new boss.

"Ms. Mason, this better be important."

I replied with a happy gloat. "If you call a chance to get an original 'Mercury' worth a cool million for only half of that important, then I guess it is."

He was silent a moment and then said, "Are you certain?"

"I spoke with the owner myself. He's in Seattle and he's agreed to see you."

"Why would he let it go at this price?"

"He wanted 600k. I told him I could get him 500k within the week."

"You're very confident with my money."

"I'm very confident in how much money this can make us both. His business is in trouble and he needs the cash."

"He told you this?"

"People tell me things. I'm a much better listener than talker."

"Indeed," he surprised me by agreeing. "Email me the details."

"I already did."

He was silent a moment. "I'll say good work if I get the painting for 500k."

"I'm looking forward to it, Mr. Compton."

If that painting sells for a million, I'll make 10 percent! It's too good to be true. How can this be my life? Of course, the auction is six months from now so I won't get my hopes up, but it's truly amazing to have the potential to make this income.

But now, it's time to think about the contract in front of me. It's long. It's scary. It's so not me, so why am I reading it?

Dr. Kat said to talk through my limits, and the first four items on the contract all bother me. That doesn't seem like a good start.

- I accept that I shall be placed in and kept under strict discipline without time limit.

Without time limit is a No Go for me.

- I accept any form of punishment meted out to me while under discipline.

What is punishment? And why the hell would I say yes? Hmmm—the flogging had been rather erotic. Is that what is meant by punishment?

- I accept any form of restraint without time limit.

No time limit is a NO.

- I agree to obey my Master in all respects. Mind, body, heart, and time belong to him.

My time belongs to him? My mind? No.

- I will have the right to operate at work, in my daily routine, without this agreement interfering. I may dress, communicate, and function as the job dictates necessary.

Well, that helps a little, but not much.

- I accept the responsibility of using my safe word when necessary, and trust implicitly in my Master to respect the use of that safe word.

This, I believe I can live with. So we have one thing I'm okay with. One. This isn't going too well.

- I will always speak of my Master in terms of love and respect. She will address him at all times as "Master."

This will take getting used to, but I'll figure it out. So I've found a second thing I can live with.

- I agree that my Master possesses the right to determine whether others can use my body and what use they may put it to.

Share me? This bothers me more than anything. How can he care about me if he wants to share me? Who would he share me with? Am I kidding myself to think he would care about me? This is sex. Just sex. In so many ways, it's what I want. No ties. No emotions. No interference in my job and career goals. Yet he wants to own my mind, time, body, and heart. It's very confusing.

• • •

*W*hat's even more confusing is that I'm not saying no to this. Why would I allow myself to be a submissive, a slave to another person?

But I know the answer: because it's him. There is something about him. What, I don't know. It's almost as if I feel like he can complete me in some way, and I'm not even sure how that is. This terrifies me. I don't want another person to be what completes me. And sharing me . . . Do I want to be shared? It's hard to imagine being with more than one person. Would I do it to please him? Would it please me? I've never thought of such a thing.

I don't think I can do this. No. I can't. I'm going to tell him no.

Friday, February 18, 2011

I didn't deal with my submissive/Master scenario today. The timing just wasn't right. I had too much going on at the gallery, and Mark was in Seattle to meet with my potential seller. I kept hoping to hear from him, but I didn't. I don't know what that means. I'm climbing the walls, wondering if he bought the painting for Riptide. Surely he knows what a big deal this is to me? But then, Mark seems to enjoy making me squirm. I must have asked Amanda a hundred times if he'd called in. I finally left him a message. He didn't call back. How am I ever going to sleep with two huge open issues?

Saturday, February 19, 2011

The minute I walked into the gallery today and found out from Amanda that Mark was in, I started for his office, only to be told that Ricco was with him. It just about made me crazy to have to wait; I've been dying to know what happened in Seattle. Then I started to worry about what Ricco and Mark might be talking about. Two hours passed and they still were in Mark's office, which made no sense to me. They don't even seem to like each other all that much. I had no idea what they could have been talking about and still don't.

When they finally came out of the office I was with a customer, and Mark and Ricco left together. Mark didn't return by the time the gallery closed and I couldn't help myself. I called him. He didn't answer. He texted me instead with: *I sent him a contract. He'll want his attorney to review it. Expect this to take weeks.*

Weeks! And a contract! I almost choked when I read that part of the message. Once again, a contract stands between me and the prize.

Monday, February 21, 2011

Chris came into the gallery to see Mark today. The two of them seem to share a mutual respect, and maybe a friendship. It's hard to tell with two such controlled men. They are so alike and so different, those two. Mark is hard on the surface, while Chris jokes with the entire staff and everyone seems to like him. But they share the same underlying strength and power. Each commands the room when he enters. I want to be like them, to be that confident, that in control. So how could I be a submissive to a Master and ever be those things? And why am I still thinking about this, when I already decided I wasn't going to sign the contract?

Tuesday, February 22, 2011

Josh showed up at the gallery today and Mark didn't seem pleased. No. That's an understatement. He was pissed. Josh actually interrupted me while I was with a customer and wanted to talk. The customer wasn't pleased. Mark ordered Mary to take over the client and directed me to his office. I can still see the gloating look on Mary's face that said she was thrilled to see me in hot water. And I was in hot water. The conversation with Mark wasn't a good one.

"Your 'boy' needs to visit on breaks or lunch, not while I have a millionaire on the floor trying to buy art."

"I didn't invite him."

"Nor have you controlled him. Deal with him, Ms. Mason. That will be all. You can leave."

Talk about feeling smacked down. He dismissed me that fast. I stood there and weighed my options. The truth seemed my only defense, so I said, "I've tried and failed. I don't understand why, but he just won't go away."

He arched a brow at me. "Are you telling me he's stalking you?"

"No. I don't want to say that, but it is getting a little creepy."

"Do I need to handle this for you?"

"God, no. I'll handle it. I will."

"But you haven't?"

"I was worried about hurting his feelings."

"So you haven't handled it at all."

"I told him I wasn't interested."

"Tell him so he knows you mean it." His voice turned to pure ice.

I didn't even know what to say to that. I simply assured him I'd handle it and started to leave.

"Ms. Mason." I paused at the door with dread in my stomach before turning back to him. "Ricco Alvarez sent you flowers. He's stopped by several times. You might not see it, but the rest of us do. He's temperamental and goes off the deep end in a blink. I do not want this ability you have to draw unstable male attention to cost me an artist."

"The flowers were a welcome to the gallery gift," I said defensively, and I immediately thought of the long meeting he'd had with Ricco. Had Ricco said something to him about me?

"No man sends roses on Valentine's Day as a welcome gift. You're smarter than that, Ms. Mason. Open your eyes."

I doubt Mark would send a woman flowers for any reason, but I bit my tongue, knowing I might regret a rebuttal later. "I'll handle Josh and Ricco." I turned to leave again and he let me.

The rest of the day, I just wanted to be out of the gallery for the first time since I started my job. When I got home, I stood in front of the mirror and stared at myself, taking in my light brown hair and green eyes. Staring at my image, I thought of Mark's comment and wondered if there was something about me that drew unstable men. Not that I think Ricco is unstable, as Mark had implied, though clearly, Josh is a little off his rocker.

And I'm not used to all this male attention. Women like Ava get male attention. She's gorgeous and I'm . . . average. The girl next door who wishes she was the beauty queen.

And here I am, sitting at my kitchen table in my oh-so-glamorous cotton PJs and eating cereal. With the contract next to me. The one thing I keep thinking is that when I was with my would-be "Master," I felt beautiful. I felt safe. I felt like I was his world. I had an escape from things like today's stresses.

That escape had to be (is?) the allure of the relationship. I've considered the punishment clause and it doesn't bother me all that much now because I do feel safe with him. Maybe that's naive, but it's how I feel. But the sharing thing—that still bothers me. What if it was with another woman? How inferior would I feel? How incapable of pleasing him?

I just need to tell him this won't work. I don't know why I haven't already.

He won't come to me, he'd said when he'd given me the contract. I have to go to him, he'd said. I have to make the willing choice to pursue him as my Master.

Wednesday, February 23, 2011

Morning . . .

I dreamed of *him*. . . . He'd tied me to his bed again, only this time I was facedown, unable to see him. I wanted to see him but I didn't feel a fear of the unknown. He wasn't touching me, but as crazy as it sounds, I could feel him. There was something about him in that dream that just reached inside me and slid straight to my soul. I had no idea what he was going to do to me. I was certain, though, that he knew best. He'd make whatever we did, whatever he did to me, pleasurable. He'd know what I needed.

I know it wasn't real, but it seemed like it was, and I've never felt that with anyone else except my mother. It's odd to compare my mother and a Master tying me to a bed, I know, but I have nothing else to compare it to. There is no one who has ever been close enough to me to gain my trust but these two people.

In the dream, and it was a dream, not a nightmare, I waited with breathless anticipation for what he would do to me. He spread me wide, his fingers sliding intimately between my thighs, stroking me, teasing me. I cannot believe how vividly I can remember the feel of him touching me. He'd been gentle in a way I didn't expect, taking me to the edge of orgasm and then abruptly withdrawing.

He'd returned to snap a crop against the mattress, making me jump. He'd warned me he wasn't going to be as gentle with me from that point forward. He'd told me it was time to leave it behind, to experience more. I'm surprised to remember how much that warning pleased me. And even more surprised at how I'd welcomed the snap of the crop on my backside, and reveled in how it became harder with each touch. I'd been shaking and panting with the sting of the leather, but I'd been aroused. And when finally (and yet too soon) it had been over, he'd kissed me from top to bottom, licking every spot he'd used the crop on. He'd been gentle again and he'd ended up between my legs, pressing my backside in the air and lapping at me until I came. And then he'd been inside me, filling me, stretching me, and it had been glorious until the dream had shifted and faded.

Suddenly I was inside my recurring nightmare of my mother, but I can't remember what happened. I just know there had been icy water, and I'd sat up in my bed gasping for air. Then the smell of my mother's perfume had permeated my nostrils. And the sense of doom I keep trying to escape returned, and now it won't go away.

To have the dream become this nightmare is unsettling. What does it mean? Is it my mind warning me that my mother betrayed me, and he will, too?

Evening . . .

I'm sitting at my kitchen table with the contract by my side and yet another box of cereal in front of me. I've just hung up from a disastrous call with Josh and I feel sick to my stomach. Since nothing else has worked, I told him I was seeing someone new and I couldn't see him anymore. He'd asked who it was and then got pretty ugly with me when I wouldn't say. I'm shocked at how he talked to me; the things he said were just unbelievable. He was nothing like the sweet guy I feared I was going to crush. His anger was downright vile. It scared me, and I don't scare easily. Really, it's been a bad day overall. I'm ready for it to be over.

Thursday, February 24, 2011

*B*efore going to work I stopped at the coffee shop, and Chris was there, sitting at a table sketching. I see him there several times a week, but I still get an adrenaline rush every time I do. He's just so damn talented and cool.

I stood in line, my eyes drawn to Chris, watching him work. It's a gift to see an artist involved in his craft. His head was down, his longish blond hair touching his collar, his expression one of deep concentration. I could have stared at him forever, watching the creative process, and didn't even realize when I was next in line until Ava joked that she often got lost watching him herself. I imagine she does.

I left and I don't think Chris even knew I was there. I was invisible. No, that's not right. He has too much control to not have known when I walked in and when I left. He simply didn't want to invite conversation or attention. I guess it's about being in his creative zone, because when he comes into the gallery, he's very friendly. But he's hard to figure out, and I didn't expect him to notice me. I never do. But . . . for some reason, today it bothered me.

Evening . . .

There were hardly any customers in the gallery, so I had to cold call and try to get people into the store. Mary was busy preparing for a private party being held at the gallery tomorrow night. She wasn't happy that I didn't want to help. I think she gets some sort of bonus for booking these events, and I think it motivates her more than the art. And it's not that I don't want to help. It's simply not a smart use of my time. Booking a ten-thousand-dollar event that we net only five thousand on doesn't equal selling one expensive piece of art. So today I was snubbed by a famous artist and Mary was irritated at me. And now I'm staring at the contract.

Somehow, I don't think tonight is the night to call my would-be "Master" and tell him I can't let him tie me up and have his wicked way with me, no matter how tempting that sounds at this moment. I'm not sure what that says about me— that I want to be tied up and at his mercy on a night I feel weak. Maybe it's what he said. That I need a safe place where I can just let go. The problem is, the contract makes that incapable of truly happening.

And on that note, I'm going to end this day the only way I can. I'm going to eat an entire bag of potato chips to go with my box of cereal. I'll regret both in the morning, but at least I'll still be in control of me.

Friday, February 25, 2011

Lunchtime . . .

*M*ark called me into his office this morning, before I left for a private showing at Ricco's gallery. I wasn't sure what to expect. I always steel myself for the impact of being alone with him. He owns you when you walk into the room. He owns you when he walks into a room. And while I'm not immune to the impact he has on everyone around him, I've often been challenged by him, eager to prove I can hold my own. Today was odd for me, because I never had a chance to do that. But it really shouldn't surprise me, I guess. I'm still rattled by the way he confronted me over Josh and Ricco.

He didn't get up from his desk. He simply steepled his fingers together and ordered, "Shut the door." I did as he said and he added, "I know you're leaving for a meeting, so I'll make this quick. You do know Ricco doesn't allow private showings?"

"No. I didn't know."

"He doesn't even allow us a full collection here."

"Why?" I asked.

"He's all about leverage. And to be clear, Ms. Mason, I will not allow him to use his art to manipulate you. We do not need his business—not with our Riptide connections. And you do not need his commissions. Not with the potential Riptide offers you."

"But you said you don't want to lose him as an artist."

"I repeat, I will not allow him to manipulate you," was his only explanation of the conflicting messages.

"I won't let him."

"I won't let him. Do you understand, Ms. Mason?"

"Yes," I whispered.

"You aren't convincing me."

"Yes," I said more clearly. "I understand."

I left his office confused and bemused. I've gone from having virtually no men in my life to being surrounded by powerful, talented, rich, controlling men, and it's messing with my head. I can't seem to figure out where I stand and where I belong.

When I took the client to Ricco's gallery, the woman didn't make a purchase and I felt embarrassed. I wanted to impress Ricco and Mark with a sale. I wanted Ricco to know I am not wasting his time. He looked at me with gentle, understanding eyes that twisted me in knots. There is nothing about him that says manipulative to me. Nothing that says he is what everyone else says he is.

I left with my client, wishing I could have stayed and talked to Ricco. I didn't call him later in the day, either, though I was tempted. I don't know what it is about him that sets everyone else off, but it doesn't happen to me. If anything, he relaxes me. Well, when I put aside how talented and famous he is.

I'm feeling very out of control. I need to figure out what is wrong with me. I have a dream job. This is what I've always wanted. I need to snap out of whatever is bugging me, and I'm hoping the weekend will give me time to think.

Saturday, February 26, 2011

Evening . . .

I decided what was bugging me was the contract, and my constant distraction due to the ideas it represents. No matter how tempting the man, the agreement is simply a deal breaker, and I think its being up in the air is influencing how I react to everything. Saying no to this contract is a good thing. This man is barely in my life and he's already taken it over. He can be in my life without taking it over if I take this off the table.

So . . . I emailed him the instant I got home, before I could talk myself out of it. The subject line was: Contract is a deal breaker. The content of the email read simply, "While you are more than a little tempting in all kinds of ways, I'm not slave material." That was an hour ago, and I keep checking my email—which is telling, isn't it? Clearly I don't want this to be over, or I'd consider it done now.

Someone just knocked on my door. It's eleven o'clock at night. Who the hell is here?

Sunday, February 27, 2011

I could barely believe it when he showed up at my door in response to my email. I just stood there, staring at him, wrapped in a robe and horrified that I had on my ugly fluffy pajamas underneath.

"Invite me in, Rebecca."

Obediently, I stepped back and let him inside. He shut the door and locked it. Now he just stood there, staring at me, and curiously, I thought I spotted a hint of uncertainty in his eyes. He's not exactly what I would call uncertain. He's not exactly what anyone would call uncertain. That I could make him feel such a thing told me what I needed to know. The outcome of what was between us wasn't simply a contract to him. I didn't realize until then how much I didn't want to be that to him.

"Let's sit," he ordered, no uncertainty left in his voice or his expression.

I wet my lips, his eyes following my tongue, and my nipples tightened and my sex clenched with the small, sensual act. With all the things that happened afterward, you'd think that would be the last thing that I'd keep replaying in my head. But it was that, along with the instant of uncertainty I'd seen in him, that told me he wanted me as much as I wanted him. These two things set the scene for what was to follow.

"Sit, Rebecca," he ordered again, and I was jolted from his spell and walked to the couch. My tiny box of an apartment embarrassed me; it's a shack compared to his gorgeous place. If he noticed, though, which of course he did, he didn't show it. He was looking at nothing but me.

He sat down on the couch, leaving the middle cushion between us free, and I got the impression he felt that I needed that space. He was right. I needed it—but I didn't want it. I wanted to be close to him. I wanted him to touch me. I always do when he's nearby.

"The contract was to be negotiated," he reminded me. "I told you that when I gave it to you."

"Yes, I know."

"Yet you simply said no."

"It felt overwhelming."

He considered me for such a long moment, I was about to go nuts. "You want this," he finally said.

"I want you," I surprised myself by admitting. I just couldn't live with the terms required to have him.

"Then you have to trust me with your pleasure."

"That contract asked for far more than my pleasure."

"And why is that bad?"

"You want too much."

"How do you define too much?"

Sharing me. "The unknowns," I said, which was still an honest answer. "I don't even understand what a lot of the things in that contract truly mean."

"And if we can take away the unknowns?"

"How can I know, when they mean nothing to me now?"

Before I knew his intent, I was on my back, and his big body was sliding over mine, the scent of him insinuating itself into my nostrils. God, I love how that man smells. I can still smell him in my apartment now as I write this.

"I'll teach you what they mean," he promised.

The idea of him teaching me was/is unbelievably arousing, as was the thick press of his erection against my stomach that assured me he wanted me that night.

Still, I have limits. And Dr. Kat had told me to tell him my limits, so I said, "There are things in that contract I'll never agree to."

"Then we take them out."

"What if they're things you want?"

"We'll negotiate. One of the best parts of the contract is openly discussing what we both want. It's about trust. You tell me what's okay. You know I won't cross that line, and you always have your safe word. You're the one in control."

"How am I in control?"

"You set the limits and we stop when you say stop. That's total control, something you don't have in a different type of relationship."

This was news to me. I hadn't thought about this relationship in that way until then.

"You have your safe word," he added. "You say it—I stop whatever I'm doing. You remember what it is?"

"Red," I said, breathless. He's good at making me breathless.

"Good," he approved and his eyes glistened with desire. "I'm going to do something I've not done in ten years. I'm going to set the contract aside for now. We'll go one lesson at a time, and I'll teach you what everything means."

Ten years? "Why would you do that?"

"Because I want you as my sub, Rebecca, like I haven't wanted another sub in a very long time. Say 'yes' and we'll go one lesson at a time. I'll be the teacher and you'll be the student."

Suddenly I had the hope I wanted, the confirmation that I wasn't just a contract. I didn't hesitate. "Yes."

I felt his instant approval, saw it in the darkening of his eyes. "Good girl."

He undressed me then, and I let him. Then, he undressed himself. I wasn't shy about watching every delicious inch of skin appear, nor was I shy about my appreciation of his jutting erection as he put on a condom.

When he came back to me, pulling me beneath him again, I was already lost in desire and ready for him. Of course, nothing is fast and simple with this man. I should have known that. "There's a few more rules," he said, and his breath was warm on my neck, his lips by my ear.

"Rules?" I asked, feeling nervous all over again, some of the haze of desire slipping away.

"You call me 'Master,' so you can get used to it."

This I could do. It was the one thing in the contract I found the least intimidating. "Yes. Okay."

"Say it." He caressed my breast and teased my nipple, as if encouraging me.

Like I would deny him his title while he was doing that to me? I'd been easy prey. "Master," I whispered with surprising comfort.

He slid down and licked my nipple. "Again," he commanded.

"Master," I panted. I've never been a panting person, but this man makes me pant. He makes me do a lot of things that I'd never do for another man.

And since he'd rewarded me for my compliance by suckling and licking my nipples, I was pretty sold on the "Master" title. If it makes him happy, apparently he'll make me happy.

Well, mostly happy. I do keep finding little things that worry me. Like how his mouth had moved to linger above mine but he hadn't kissed me. And I realized that he hasn't kissed me many times at all.

"You will call me 'Master' when we're alone," he instructed next. (Still no kiss.) "In public, we remain as we are. What we are beyond that is between us."

My heart sank. My conclusion then, and now, is that he wants to basically own me without claiming me. And how am I to separate the times we meet for work with this?

I'd been back to feeling like there was a contract, but he'd distracted me. His mouth had gone back to my nipple, his tongue swirling and teasing. His cock slid against my slick, swollen body, and I forgot what we were talking about for a few minutes.

Only the talk wasn't over. "Final rule," he said, teasing me with the promise he was going to enter me to the point I couldn't think. "Until we sign our contract, your safe word is everything. Use it liberally. Use it, and I'll stop whatever I'm doing. Say it now."

"But I don't want you to stop."

He laughed, soft and wicked, the first time I've ever heard him laugh. "I just want to know that you know what it is."

"I do."

"Use it and no matter what we are doing, no matter how intense it is, no matter where we are, I'll end whatever we are doing. You have my word. But you won't need it tonight. I'll guarantee it."

And oh, how true that guarantee had been. My "Master" proceeded to show me a side of himself I wouldn't have believed existed. I hesitate to say that he made love to me, because "love" is a word that scares the hell out of me. And he's not a man to fall in love with. I've been reminding myself of that fact ever since I met him.

So maybe he didn't make love to me, but it didn't feel like fucking, either. There were no floggers. There were no ropes or ties. Just his mouth, his hands, and my pleasure. He didn't ask anything of me, but . . . he didn't let me touch him, either. It was all about him touching me—not that I can complain. I've never felt like I did last night. Every lick, from my nipples to my clit, was a soft, delicious, seductive stroke that turned me inside out.

But he also left in the wee hours of the morning, leaving me alone in bed. It had felt bad. Alone has always felt safe, not bad, so I'm not sure what it means that it no longer does.

Maybe it's the nightmares messing with me. Maybe it's my worst fear—that he's going to make me forget how to be alone. Yet didn't he quickly remind me I am alone?

Worse, I've agreed to lessons on how to be submissive, but I have no idea when we will have our meeting. He promised to be in touch. I am totally at his mercy.

He says I have ultimate control. This does not feel like control.

Monday, March 7, 2011
Nearly lunchtime . . .

After a sleepless night, I headed to the coffee shop before work. Ava was chatty. She wants to talk men and personal lives every time she sees me, and I've never felt less like connecting with someone else about my personal life than I do now. I prefer to write down my thoughts. Writing lets me think out what I feel without anyone else influencing me, and that isn't likely to change. I'm beginning to want to avoid the coffee shop. In a space of ten minutes, Ava has asked me about Ricco, Mark, Chris, and another artist who apparently comes into the gallery sometimes, but hasn't since I arrived.

While I was still there, the client I took to Ricco's private gallery called my cell phone to see if she could take a relative by to see a work she was thinking of buying. Ava was all over my reaction, which was pure dread, and wanted to know what was wrong.

I didn't tell her. She truly was nothing but friendly, but I don't even share my worries and concerns with long-term friends. Besides, she's gorgeous and composed, ten years older than me, and apparently from a wealthy family, from what she said today. What do we have in common?

Oh, right. The men in our lives that she knows well and I don't. Finding out that she has bedded, or could bed, all of them won't help me. In fact, it might really mess with my head. I'd rather not know.

When I arrived at the gallery, it took me half an hour to

make the dreaded call to Ricco to ask to drop by with my customer. I kept thinking about Mark telling me that Ricco never does private showings, and how this would probably feel very intrusive to him.

What if he refused? I'd have an unhappy customer and an unhappy artist, which meant an unhappy Mark. An unhappy Mark isn't on my list of things to do, any more than wasting Ricco's time again is. I was actually relieved to get Ricco's voicemail and be forced to leave a message.

But what made me open my journal right now to write is Mary. She's bothering me beyond her basic bitchiness, and something very odd happened today with her. She was in Mark's office for about fifteen minutes and then stormed by my office in an obvious hissy fit. Apparently she left the gallery, and no one knows where she is. I'd thought from the beginning that her job was on the line, but since then I've gained respect for how well she handles the special events. I'm just not sure she wants to handle them. Maybe the new intern who started today was brought in to replace that part of her job, and I'm handling the sales aspect?

I have a customer. More later.

Evening ...

I'm still in disbelief. I can't believe I did what I did today. In a public place! After I finished with my customer, Mary returned to the gallery all smiley and happy, in a way she never acts. I'm not sure what that means, but when I volunteered to pick up sandwiches for me, Amanda, the new intern, and Ralph, she not only wanted to join us, she offered to pick them up. A very odd offer from her, and way too nice to fit her personality. Somehow, though, the sandwiches turned to pizza, so I headed to the sandwich shop on my own.

Truth be told, I needed some fresh air. All morning I'd been thinking about Saturday night, and how I'd actually said "Yes, Master" in hopes of being rewarded with another lick or flick or touch, when I should have been focused on work. And when I wasn't thinking about sex today, I was overanalyzing everything in my life in a way I've never done before.

I have my dream job, and I'm distracted, which I would never have thought possible. Everything used to be so simple. I wanted to work in the art world, and I drove my life toward that. Then my mother died and I had to pay the bills, so I drove my life toward that. I was in control of what I was doing, even if I wasn't happy about the direction I was headed. Now, I'm in this complicated web but still living a dream, and it's unfamiliar and strange, but exciting. And control? After today, I can say with certainty that it is lost.

Which brings me back to the crazy thing I let myself do. I braved the chilly San Francisco weather to walk the several blocks to the deli, all bundled up. Everything was so normal when I entered the small restaurant. I ordered an egg salad sandwich and sat down at one of the small tables by the door with my food and my journal, intending to start this entry. That's when my cell phone buzzed with a text from him. Go into the bathroom it read.

Adrenaline rushed through me to the point that I could barely catch my breath. He was here? How was that possible?

No, I told myself; he didn't say he was here. He just ordered me to the bathroom. Who knew what kind of mind games he played as "Master"? I was in new territory. Knowing this, I pulled myself together and calmed down. But I was eager to discover what he wanted.

Quickly, I stood up and headed to the bathroom, leaving my lunch on the table. The sign led me down a narrow hall to the left where there were two unisex doors. I took a guess, opened the first door, and went inside. He was there, looking deliciously him. (How else do you describe perfection?) Heat poured through me and settled in my belly.

He stepped forward, removing the small space between us, towering above me. "Put your purse on the counter," he ordered softly.

I shoved it onto the counter I hadn't even looked at. Who cares what the bathroom looks like when he's in it?

"What were you supposed to reply to my order, Rebecca?" he asked, and there was no missing the warning in his voice.

It took me a moment to process, but I remembered what I'd been taught Saturday night, how I'm to reply to everything he commands. "Yes, Master."

"Take off your panties."

The order aroused me like I'd never been aroused, but then, I say that about a lot of things with this man. I also do a lot of things willingly I'd have never thought I would. "Yes, Master," I replied again, and the heated approval in his eyes was like a stroke of his hand over my already aching sex.

I tugged the skirt of my pencil-cut black dress up to my hips and slipped my tiny black thong down my legs and over my high heels. When I started to tug down my hem, he ordered me to leave it up so that I was bared for his viewing. I complied and gave him another "Yes, Master."

Then I dared to dangle my panties by my finger, because, well, what else was a girl going to do in that situation? He took them from me and, without touching me, stuffed them in his pocket. I knew I wasn't getting them back. He'd have that little part of me with him the rest of the day and I'd be bare, thinking of him and what we wouldn't have time to do in a public bathroom. The panties ensured that he would, too.

"Unzip your dress and let me see your nipples," he ordered next. Someone knocked on the door and he added, "Ignore them. Do as I said."

I can't believe, knowing where I was, how busy the deli was, that I didn't hesitate. I reached for my zipper. "Stop," he said, and he did not sound pleased.

My heart lurched at the hard-spoken word and I froze, staring at him an instant before I knew what he wanted. "Yes, Master," I said quickly.

He inclined his chin and I tugged down the front of my dress, then shoved my bra out of the way. His gaze swept downward, over my aroused nipples, and I reacted so completely, feeling him all over and burning for him to touch me and be inside me, that he might as well have physically touched me all over. I'd never wanted any man like I wanted this man in that bathroom.

His gaze lifted from my breasts and held mine. "Touch them," he ordered as someone jiggled the door handle behind me.

This time, I ignored the person trying to get in. "Yes, Master." I touched my nipples and teased them and his hot stare was my reward.

"Good," came his approval (another reward), but it was followed by what felt like punishment. He stepped back, putting more space between us, then leaned on the wall and crossed his arms over his broad chest. "Make yourself come."

"I can't here," I gasped, and the floor just about fell out from underneath me. "People want the bathroom."

"You can and you will."

The door jiggled again. "I'll be out in a minute!" I snapped impatiently. He arched an amused brow at my outburst, seemingly unaffected by the intrusion. But then, he wasn't the one who had to make himself come while people demanded entry.

"The sooner you come," he told me, "the sooner we walk out of here."

I'd never masturbated for a man before and surely not in a public place, but as panicked as I felt in that moment, I never doubted I was going to do what he wanted. I'm not sure what that says about me or how about he affects me. Not only did I know I was going to do it, I was so damn aroused by the idea that I was burning up, hot and weak in the knees all over again. I knew we couldn't get caught. We might get yelled at for being in the bathroom, but no one could prove we had done anything but talk. That comforted me. I could be naughty with him, for him, but I wasn't going to get in trouble.

I drew a breath, issued my "Yes Master," spread my legs wider, and slid my fingers down to my clit to stroke. I watched him watch me, encouraged by the darkening of his eyes, as I explored the silky wet heat of my arousal. His watching me made me wetter, hotter, more needy. Pleasure overtook me, lowering my lashes, and I let it, ripples of sensation weakening my knees, and I orgasmed with amazing speed. When I finally opened my eyes again, he was standing in front of me.

"You're meant for this, Rebecca, and you looked exquisite, coming like that." He slid a finger between my legs and then sucked it into his mouth. "And now I'll have you on my lips the rest of the day."

He reached for the door and I quickly pulled my clothes together, but by the time I did he was gone. I snatched my purse up as a woman walked in and gasped when she realized I'd been inside the room with a man. I hurried out into the hallway and to my table, expecting my "Master" would be waiting. But he wasn't there.

I gathered my coat and sandwich and quickly headed for the gallery, where I spent the afternoon excruciatingly aware of my pantyless state. That was what he'd planned, what he wanted.

I don't buy into me having all the control just because I have a safe word. I have no control where this man is concerned. That should make me run for the hills, but I know I'm not going anywhere except where he leads me. I hope that isn't a mistake, but I can't find the will to care.

Wednesday, March 9, 2011
Lunchtime at my desk . . .

Ricco was not only fine with the private showing, he didn't seem upset at all, which is a relief. I hope the client calls me back soon, because I've left Ricco in limbo about when we are coming by. He is tolerant now, but how long will that last?

Okay . . . Mary just popped into my office and asked if I needed anything while she was out. This can't be the same woman who all but called me a whore. Have I entered an alternate universe where she got some sort of fairy wings handed to her?

Almost time to go home . . .

Seven o'clock and it's time to pack up to leave the gallery. No call from my client about visiting Ricco's gallery. To top that off, there has been no erotic "Master" encounter today and I am disappointed. But then, I guess he's not my Master yet, so I shouldn't expect a daily demand from him. Should I once he's my Master? I mean IF he's my Master. The contract makes me think he pretty much intends to dictate to me daily. Hmmm . . . this makes me think, and I don't like where my head is going. Does he have another submissive right now? Will he have more than one when he's with me? The contract does talk about sharing me with others. Oh, God. This idea upsets me. I have to text him. Or should I call him? Texting is less intimidating. I'll text. Maybe. I need to go home and think about this.

At home now . . .

Thinking has made me certain I need an answer. If I am one of many submissives, then this is over. I'm going to text. That

way, if I find out I'm one of many, I can flip out in the privacy
of my apartment.

Thursday, March 10, 2011

Work came early today since I basically didn't sleep last night.
So much has happened since I sent that text to my would-be
"Master." He replied immediately and told me he was sending
a car to pick me up so we could talk. He didn't ask if he could
send a car. He just told me he was.

I remember sitting there reading the text, and it wasn't the
order that bothered me. It was the fact that he hadn't simply
said that I was the only woman he was with at present. I'd considered texting again and asking, but my gut said he wouldn't
reply until I went to him. I replied that I'd be waiting for the
car.

I didn't change clothes or pretty myself up while I waited
for my ride to arrive. I left on my navy blue sheath dress from
work. I wanted answers, not sex, and that was the message I set
out to deliver. The possibility of being one of several women
had really changed everything for me. I don't know why, but
that idea had hit me far harder than the idea of being shared. I
didn't like either, but I *really* didn't like being just a number and
a contract.

When the car dropped me at his home, I headed down the
walkway. The instant I lifted my hand to knock, he appeared in
the doorway. Seeing him sent a rush of heat through me and froze
me in place. I always react to that first instant I see him, but for

some reason it was more intense than usual. Maybe because I'd decided that I might walk away from what he'd been offering me.

I searched his expression, but if he felt what I did, it didn't show. His face was impassively beautiful, as usual, and I wondered how many times he'd had to calm a potential submissive. What number was I for him?

He surprised me by taking my hand, touching me easily, when his touch always feels like a reward to be earned. Guiding me into the foyer, he shut the door and then turned to me, wasting no time answering my question from the earlier text. "The contract states exclusivity for both of us, with the option of bringing others into our play as I see fit."

My stomach knotted at the confirmation that he intended to invite others into our play, and I tried to pull my hand back.

He held me easily and I found myself molded close to him, the hard length of him pressed to my body, our legs entwined. His hand had settled on my back, possessive and firm. "What did I say that upset you?"

My fingers curled on his chest. "Exclusive and sharing. How do those two things go together?"

"Everything we enjoy, we enjoy together. And ultimately, everything I do with you is about your pleasure."

"And if I don't think sharing is pleasurable?"

"How do you know if you don't try?"

"I know it bothers me."

"And I ask you to try everything once. If you don't like it, we won't repeat it."

Once? I wasn't sure I could say yes. I don't think I would have, if things had been different, but I had no idea what I'd walked into.

"If this is your worst fear," he said, "then it's better that we deal with it now, not later." He released me, the warmth of his body leaving mine, his fingers twining with mine. I let him lead me to the bedroom when perhaps I shouldn't have. It was there that I quickly learned what I had in store.

There was another man there—tall and gorgeous, dark where my "Master" was light, wearing jeans and a T-shirt that molded a perfectly sculpted body. To say that my heart lurched is an understatement. I could barely breathe.

My Master stepped behind me, his hands settling possessively at my waist, his lips lowering to my ear. "Try it once. Do this for me."

"I don't know," I whispered, surprising myself. I hadn't said no—I'd said maybe.

"You have your safe word," he immediately replied. "Use it and we stop."

Thinking back now, the most profound moments of the night followed that promise from him. Everything had gone into slow motion. My Master's hands on my body, caressing my sides, my breasts. The other man, whose name I still don't know, watching me with a heated, anxious expression on his face.

"One time," my Master whispered. "I just ask for one time."

I remember wanting to please him, or telling myself that was what I wanted, and then saying yes.

"Good girl," he murmured, and the other man had smiled and stepped forward. Before I had time to back out, the stranger was sliding his hands to my waist, his thighs melded to mine. It seemed like in a blink of time all three of us were naked. I have these random memories. Me on my knees. My Master behind me, holding my breast. The stranger licking my nipples. The stranger pressing fingers inside me. Both men inside me at the same time. I'd never dreamed that was possible, or that it could be pleasurable. Those two men together . . .

I can't deny it *was* pleasurable, yet I'm still bothered by how easily my Master allowed another man to touch me. I can't be special to him, or he'd want me all to himself, right? I don't want to share him with another woman. It's all so very confusing . . . and though I have time to try new things while I decide if I am going to sign the contract, I don't like this state of limbo, or the way exclusivity begins only after I sign the contract. I need closure and certainty sooner rather than later.

Friday, March 11, 2011

*T*oday my job took over in the most wonderful way, and I was able to quickly forget about the contract. I started out the morning with a sale. It wasn't a big one, but it was still a sale. I set up the meeting with Ricco and my client for Monday. The most exciting part, though, was Chris coming by the gallery and my being called into Mark's office. I soon forgot about being nervous when I heard the reason I was there. Chris set up a charity event for next month with us, and he's going to unveil a new work that will later be auctioned off at Riptide for his charity. Mark and Chris asked me to organize it, instead of Mary, since it's attached to Riptide.

I am beyond elated! A new work from Chris? People will

be fighting for tickets to see him unveil a new work. This is so exciting, and I'm eager to dig into the details tomorrow.

As for my decision to be submissive, well, I've been reading up on the internet on BDSM and I've been tuning in to the Dr. Kat show quite often. I'm thinking about calling her again. I need someone who understands the dynamics of the Master/sub relationship, and I like the anonymity of calling in.

Aside from that, I'm supposed to have another lesson tomorrow night at his place. I just hope there are only two of us—not three.

Saturday, March 12, 2011

Morning . . .

The nightmare came back. I *hate* that damn nightmare. I hate how real the icy water feels, pouring into my lungs. And I hate my mother's perfume, which I used to love. That sense of doom is back. I hadn't even realized it had left until it returned. At least tonight, I'll be lost in some kind of sexual fantasy sure to make me forget. Escaping into his world sounds very good right now.

Sunday, March 13, 2011

Last night I went to his house for a lesson, and it was just the two of us. It was sexy and amazing. He tied me up and produced a pair of nipple clamps. I'd never been clamped and it hurt at first, but it was sweet bliss once the ache faded. He'd told me he was my escape, my place where I could let the rest of the world fade away. And it did. It was one of the few times in my life that I have ever fully let go. I didn't think; I just let myself get lost in what I felt. He'd made me feel that safe.

But then he'd sent me home with a driver, and I crashed hard and felt alone all over again. The kind of alone that feels bad.

I think I'm already falling for him. I think I could fall in love with him. But is a man who is all about Master and sub capable of falling in love? Could he ever be happy with just me? There are moments when I see something in his eyes, when I feel something in his touch, and I believe he already does. When he sent me home, I almost thought it was because he wanted to escape what he felt. But that might just be me hoping for more than a contractual arrangement.

I don't want to set myself up for heartbreak, but maybe it's too late to avoid. Maybe I am destined to have my heart ripped to pieces by this man—because I know as I write this that I can't walk away from him. I need to sign the contract and put the uncertainty and worry aside. I thought about calling in to the Dr. Kat show, hoping she would talk me out of such a rash action, but I know she won't. I've made up my mind. I'm going to sign the contract.

And whatever will be, will be.

Rebecca's Lost Journals Vol. 3:
His Submissive

Journal 6, entry 1

Monday, March 14 , 2011

7:00 a.m.

I, Rebecca Mason, belong to him, my new Master. Or I will as soon as I sign the contract he's given me to set the terms for our Master/sub relationship.

I woke a few minutes ago with these thoughts, and now, sitting at the kitchen table of my little San Francisco apartment, excitement is running through me. Now that I've decided to sign the contract, the idea of being "his" is downright intoxicating. Still, I'm glad I was the cautious girl that I am, and made myself sleep on the decision. Considering my recent nightmares, my good night's rest speaks loudly. I'm at peace with my decision to sign the contract.

Still, how crazy is it for me to feel this confident about giving myself to someone else? Only a few weeks ago, I would have never believed this possible. Before "him," the idea of being submissive to anyone simply wasn't comprehensible. All my life has been about learning from my single mother to control my own destiny and stand on my own two feet. Handing over complete control to another person simply wasn't an option . . . until him. Now, how do I tell him I'm signing our contract? A text? A call? Meet him in person? Hmmm . . . off to shower and think about this . . .

*W*hile I was in the shower, I came up with the perfect way to tell him I'm his. First, the right attire. I've dressed in a sexy pale pink dress the color of spring roses, one that hugs my curves (to get his attention) without being overly sexy for work. It's also perfect for an event being held at the gallery tonight. I just have to throw on a little lace jacket I recently purchased to spice it up.

Next, I took the big plunge and inked the contract. I then slipped on the beautifully designed ring with an etched rose he'd given me to wear after signing the contract, as a symbol that I am his. So it's on my finger and I keep sitting here staring at it, expecting fear or regret, but I feel none. I feel right about this.

It's crazy how my life has changed in a matter of weeks. I dared to chase my dream of working in the art world, taking a low-paying job at the gallery that required me to work a second job to pay the bills. Then, miraculously, that gamble paid off with a chance to earn big commissions through Mark's auction house. I have a new career, and I'm discovering a new, daring part of me, a part I can't wait to explore further. And I have "him." Or I will by the end of today.

All that is left now is for me to take a picture of both the contract and the ring on my finger. Then I'll text the photos to him. Okay . . . done. Photos taken. I'm about to send the text messages. I'm nervous and excited. This is it. I'm really doing this.

Almost 1:00 p.m. and my lunchtime

I haven't seen or heard from "him" since I texted the pictures. Not a word. This decision was huge for me, and I thought he'd know that and respond. I feel uncertain. I feel . . . confused. The gallery I normally love feels like a prison I need to escape. I'm leaving for lunch just to get out of here, though I know I won't be able to eat. I guess I'll walk to the chocolate shop and buy about ten pounds of the best they have, go to the coffee shop for caffeine, and then pig out. Chocolate isn't food; it's a drug meant to cure all. It should make me feel better, at least while I'm consuming it. There will be regret afterward, but if it's the only regret I feel today, I'm okay with that.

2:00 p.m.

Back at the gallery in my office . . .

I saw him, my would-be, should-be-already Master, who is twisting me in knots. The chocolate/coffee plan turned into the encounter with him I'd been waiting on all morning. After I bought my chocolate, I headed straight to the coffee shop, where I found a corner booth (and hoped to dodge Ava, the chatty owner of the place who is always trying to dig up gallery gossip from me).

I'd just settled into my seat when the air shifted around me, telling me he'd stepped into the shop even before I saw him. I always know when he's around. There's this subtle energy that seems to crackle in the air, and I know I'm not the only person who feels it. I can see how the gazes around me seek him out, how attention finds him.

My nerves went haywire at the knowledge he was there. My stomach fluttered and my heart raced so quickly, I actually felt faint.

I keep replaying the moment he came into view and stole my breath, as he always does. Tall and broad, he sauntered toward me with sleek, feline grace, and I had the sense he was stalking his prey and that prey was me. His eyes found mine, or maybe mine found his, and the hardness in their depths had actually made my chest hurt. He affects me that much, like no other man, or anyone, ever has. He was angry. I had no idea why, but he was angry. I knew then what his silence had already told me; I just didn't want to admit it. I'd dared to open myself up to him and he was going to reject me.

I had to cut my gaze away from his in an effort to recover my lost composure. I rarely feel out of sorts in such a way. My skin tingled and almost burned as he neared, closing in on me, and I cursed my inability to control my physical response to him. I can still feel the dread that filled me, paralyzed me, when he stopped by my table, towering above me.

"Look at me," he demanded softly, but there was no softness to the command.

I forced my gaze back to his and those hard eyes were still hard. Still angry. Some part of me had hoped that I'd read him wrong moments before.

I didn't speak. I couldn't speak. I simply had no idea what to say; I didn't even fully understand what I felt.

"You don't sign the agreement or put on the ring until I say you're ready," he said in a low, commanding reprimand.

I was stunned. This wasn't a rejection. It was a . . . I didn't know what. "But you tried to convince me to sign—"

"To be open to signing," he corrected. "And then, only when I say you're ready—not a moment before."

"I am ready," I declared.

He leaned down, hands pressed to the table in front of me, his erotic scent teasing my nostrils. He leveled me in a stare, and that cruel, amazing mouth of his was so near I could feel his hot breath on my lips. "No," he said tightly. "You are not ready and clearly you still don't understand the rules. But you will. Take off the ring until I say otherwise."

My chest had tightened to the point of misery. I remember thinking, "Do I really want to be with someone who can make me feel pain so easily?" But as much as I knew what my answer should be, I heard myself ask him, "Are you serious?"

"Do I ever say anything I don't mean?"

I stared at him for several seconds and decided that no, he did not. I took off the ring. When I tried to hand it to him he said, "Keep it, but you don't wear it until I say you can." His lips thinned. "Now. Let's go to the bathroom and finish this conversation."

My mind immediately raced. Who was in the coffee shop? Who would see us go to the bathroom as a pair? "What if someone sees us?"

He just stared at me, the look on his face as steely as any

I'd ever seen. He fully intended for me to do as he wished. I knew that if I didn't, this thing between us would end there and then.

With my fingers curled around the ring, the sharp corners digging into my tender flesh, I stood up. He straightened with me and somehow I resisted the urge to scan for who might be watching us. He stepped backward, giving me just enough space to pass him, and I was thankful we were so close to the back of the shop and the bathroom that perhaps we wouldn't be seen together. It was the facade I needed to be able to move forward.

Once I managed to walk, I quickly cut to my left and down a small hall before rushing into the bathroom. My awareness of his joining me in the small space was instant; the tiny box of a room suddenly made me feel like a caged animal, wild and uncertain. My emotions were a jumble of uncontrollable knots that he was pulling tighter.

I heard the lock seal us inside, and I started to turn when he grabbed me and pressed me against the sink. My fingers curled around the white ceramic as he yanked my snug-fitted dress up my hips. Then he was at my side, his thick erection resting on my hip, his fingers sliding between my thighs, under the black silk of my thong. But what stilled my heart and then set it racing was the way the palm of his other hand began to caress my bare backside.

"Do you know why you aren't ready?" he asked, his head resting against mine, his fingers doing a delicious slide over my clit.

"I am ready," I declared—and while I tried to sound firm, my voice was a raspy whisper.

"No," he insisted. "You aren't ready because you don't

understand the rules." He slipped two fingers inside me and I panted at the intimate invasion, ripples of pleasure pulsing through me, as he added, "You don't do anything unless I say you do it. That especially applies to signing the contract."

"I thought—"

"Did you?" he challenged, flicking my clit with his thumb. "I'm not sure you did."

I opened my mouth to reply but one of his hands still caressed my backside, and the strokes became rougher, his fingers kneading into my flesh. Sudden realization overcame me. He was going to spank me. I knew it and it terrified and aroused me. I didn't know how that was possible then, any more than I do now as I write this.

"Did you read every line of the document, Rebecca?"

"Yes." I barely whispered the reply due to the sensations ravishing my body. His hand was still stroking my backside, his fingers stroking inside me.

"Then you must understand that acting without my permission comes with punishment."

"I-I didn't think . . . I—"

"Exactly. You have to learn to think. You cannot be a sub, my sub, and not understand the rules and the consequences of misbehaving. I intend to give you a lesson on those things, Rebecca. Do you want that lesson?"

No. Yes. What lesson? "You mean now, or . . . ?"

"Now," he said firmly.

Looking back now, I should have said "no" or asked questions. I didn't. I felt pressured to do as he wished, and his fingers were doing delicious things to my body. Actually, I'm lying to myself. I don't think I felt pressured at all. I think I wanted to know what he would do to me. The truth is that all I was really thinking was to say "yes" so his fingers would keep doing exactly what they were doing in the exact spot they were in.

"Yes," I gasped, and his fingers sent wicked, wonderful sensations spiraling through me. "I want the lesson."

"Yes, what?" he demanded.

"Yes, Master."

Instead of rewarding me for my agreement with the orgasm I so desired, his fingers stopped teasing me, sliding away so that his hand rested on my pelvis. I wanted to cry out, to demand satisfaction, but I was stayed by the way his palm on my backside stilled and flexed into my skin.

"I'm going to spank you, Rebecca," he declared, "and you need to know that I will do it again, or use other forms of punishment if we move forward beyond today and you fail to follow our rules. Understand?"

No. No, I did not. I was scared and confused, but I was also aroused and curious. I wanted him. I want him even now, no matter how much he's twisted me in knots. I knew I couldn't turn back.

"Yes. I understand." I'd barely issued the approval when his hand came down hard. I gasped as the sensation rocked me, and I struggled to identify what I felt. My stomach knotted with the sting of my flesh that spiraled through me, and then, to my shock, tightened my sex. The rest of the punishment was fast and hard, ten full contacts of his palm, I think, all of which were harder, stronger. I had a moment when I was confused by the pleasure rippling through me and I thought I should object, I should scream my safe word, "red," but my voice was swollen in my throat, and any protest with it.

The assault of his hand stopped suddenly and his fingers slid back between my thighs, and I was shocked that I was slick and wet and aroused. It was beyond belief, considering what he'd just done to me. But I was, and when he slipped his fingers back inside me and stroked my swollen flesh, I shattered almost instantly. It was breathtakingly good. He'd spanked me and I had one of the best orgasms ever, but I'd recovered angry and confused. Embarrassed. I still am.

"I will never leave you with anything but pleasure," he murmured. "Remember that."

"And I will never go to another public bathroom with you," I ground out. "This is the last time."

His response was to gently pull my dress back into place and then turn me to face him. "You will if I say you will."

His tone was matter-of-fact, as if he didn't even acknowledge my anger. And then he stepped back and gave me space.

Both pissed me off more than ever, and I blasted him, "People I work with come here, and I have to walk out there and pretend I didn't just do what we did!" The sharp edges of the ring dug into my palm, reminding me I still held it. I stepped toward him, grabbed his hand, and shoved the ring into his palm. "Anything near my work is off limits. That's a hard limit for me. Put it in your damn contract."

He captured my hand before I could escape. "That's what I was looking for. Real thought. Real negotiation. An agreement you don't just live with, but embrace."

He released me and I felt shell-shocked. He'd pushed me

intentionally, intending to force me to see what I'd missed when making my decision to sign the agreement.

"Now," he said, "you can put the ring back on if you still think you're ready."

He didn't wait for an answer because he knew I wasn't. He headed to the door and exited.

I stood there for I don't know how long, my thoughts a jumbled mess, before I forced myself to exit regardless of who might see me. There was only Ava, who stared at me with unabashed interest.

I rushed to my table and grabbed my things before heading back to the gallery to put my thoughts on paper.

My backside still burns, and it reminds me that this decision to give myself to him does come with consequences, just as disobeying him apparently does. Yes, those consequences seem to arouse me, but I barely recognize this person that is me, who finds a spanking hot and sexy.

But I did. I do. I'm scared to death that I'm losing touch with myself. Am I truly ready for this relationship?

The ring is sitting on my desk and I haven't put it back on. I'm not sure I'm going to. I'm not even sure I'm allowed to. I dread tonight's event, one that I would normally look forward to. It's a huge open house for Georgia O'Nay, a brilliant local artist receiving critical acclaim. It's an exciting event with an impressive list of attendees, but all I can think is that everyone who is anyone will be here, including him.

I'd actually rather go home and think and process where I'm headed in this new life, rather than attend a magical art showing.

What is happening to me?

Midnight
Finally home . . .

$\mathcal{G}$eorgia O'Nay is thirty-five, with long, sleek black hair and gorgeous pearl-like skin, and the talent of a goddess. It didn't surprise me that she drew a wall-busting crowd. The event had spectacular desserts, expensive champagne, and great art. It was pure heaven for art lovers. It should have been for me, but it wasn't.

All the local artists who show in the gallery were present. Ricco Alvarez and Chris Merit were crowd favorites. Chris, unlike the rest of the guests, who were in suits (Ricco included), was a rebel in jeans and a leather jacket. When he stood next to Mark, the contrast in the two men was extreme but the power and sex radiating off them both was overwhelming.

It bothered me that "he" spent a lot of time by Georgia's side. I tried not to let it. I really did. In my defense, I was feeling insecure after the entire ring situation. But what really set me off was the concrete block of realization that hit me as I admired her work. Georgia paints flowers. Roses mostly. Yes. Roses. How could I not connect his attention to her to the design of the ring? How could anyone not in a similar situation? Had she been his sub at some point? Did he help her launch her career? And if so, what happened between them? Why did they part ways? Or had they parted ways? Am I just a side dish?

During one moment when the two of them appeared rather intimate, my stomach actually churned. I wondered then, again, what was happening to me. How had I gone from being the girl who needed no one to feeling such intense need for one man? I suddenly felt that this new life was controlling me, not the other way around.

Needing air, I rushed for the back door. The instant I stepped outside into the chilly San Francisco night, I inhaled deeply, yet I still felt like I couldn't breathe. I hugged myself, the little lace vest I'd put on for the evening doing nothing to warm me.

Then the door opened behind me and I whirled around, shocked to see him standing there. And damn him, no matter how inadequate he'd made me feel inside the gallery, his presence still washed over me with a consuming, all-powerful burn. I resented it, not wanting him to have that power over me.

Before I knew his intention, he pulled me around a corner so that we were out of the line of sight of the door. He pressed me against the wall, the warm glow of a lamp fixture casting us in its light, his thighs hugging mine. His fingers framed my face. "You're upset. I don't want you to be upset."

"Funny," I said bitterly, "I didn't think what I felt mattered to you."

His thumb caressed my cheek. "Ah, little one, you've become confused. As your Master, my greatest desire and responsibility is your pleasure, happiness, and safety. To upset you is to fail you. In this agreement you will make me your world, but I, too, will make you my world. Now," he said, stroking the hair from my face, "tell me what's wrong."

For the second time today, embarrassment assailed me. I buried my face in his chest but he wasn't letting me escape. He lifted my face, forcing my gaze back to his. "Tell me what's wrong, Rebecca."

My hands went to his hands and he let me touch him. So

often, he doesn't. It calmed me enough to confess my feelings. "Everything. Everything is wrong. You didn't contact me all morning and I was in knots wondering what you thought. Then you made me take the ring off. Do you know what a big deal it was for me to have signed that contract? Do you know how much it ripped me apart when you rejected what I offered you?"

"No matter how much I want you to be mine, to let you sign when you aren't ready would be assuring our agreement will fail. I don't intend to let that happen."

His voice was raspy, thick with emotion, and I want to believe he feels something for me. Actually, I know he feels something for me. But what does a man like him feel? A need to possess some new toy, and I'm that toy? Perhaps even a passionate need to possess that toy? And while I'm no Cinderella looking for a Prince Charming, nor a damsel looking for a hero, while standing there with him, I had a sense that I will always want more from him than he will give me.

"Why didn't you just say you wanted me to understand more, rather than taking me in that bathroom today?" I asked, trying to understand him.

"Because while I am willing to give you more time before you sign the agreement, I admit that I am impatient to make our agreement official. Before that happens, you have to understand what's in the contract, including the rules."

"And the punishments," I added.

"Yes. And the punishments."

"How . . . intense does punishment get?"

He stared down at me, his eyes searching mine, and then

he shocked me by leaning in and tenderly brushing his lips over mine. "As I said in the bathroom, I will push you to your limit, Rebecca, but I will always leave you thoroughly pleasured."

The gentleness in him, contrasting the hardness I so often saw, softened my worries, but there was still one thing I couldn't let go. "And Georgia. Did you leave her thoroughly pleasured?"

He pulled back to stare at me, genuine shock on his face. "Georgia?"

"She paints roses. Was the ring once hers? And are you still involved with her? Because if you are, I'm done. I won't be—"

He laughed, a sexy, surprising sound from a man so serious. "No, little one. It was never her ring. I've never been intimate with Georgia, nor do I intend to be." His voice softened and his gaze heated to scorching. "Just you, Rebecca. This relationship will be exclusive as long as we have a written agreement. Understand?"

I nodded, but I wasn't totally relieved. We would never be exclusive when he was willing to share me.

"And even if it kills me in the process," he continued, "we'll take this slowly, as I intended. I'll teach you what each point in the contract means. Then we will negotiate the final terms. But know this. When you put that ring back on, there will be no holding back for either of us. You will belong to me."

But will he belong to me? And why was I afraid to ask?

Probably because, deep down, I know the answer . . . and I don't want to accept it. This powerful man will never belong to anyone.

He stroked my cheek again, tenderness in the touch. "We should get back before we're missed," he said, and I agreed.

An hour later, I ended up huddled in a chat with Mark and three amazing artists. Could I really be standing with Ricco Alvarez, Chris Merit, and Georgia O'Nay? Chris, Mark, and I chatted a bit about a charity event that I'm handling for Chris, and we set up a meeting for the next day. Remarkably, considering my first reaction to her presence, I bonded with Georgia quickly, much as I had with Ricco, and she turned out to be as nice as she was talented and beautiful. I think I just get artists. I connect with them. Despite all that Mark does for the art world, I'm not sure he always does.

I took a cab home at the gallery's expense. The entire staff did since Mark won't let anyone drive after a gallery event that includes alcohol, and this one had. I'd barely walked in the door when my would-be Master texted me.

You decide when the next lesson is. Call me when you're ready.

I don't know when I'll be ready. Part of me says now. Part of me says I might never be. Yet I'd been downright excited to sign the contract this morning. Now I'm not sure of anything.

Wednesday, March 16, 2011

Hot bath. Pajamas. My own bed. What more could I want? Ah, but I know: him. I want to call him. I want to hear his voice and I want . . . so much. But it's the wrong choice. I know this. I've been singing this song to myself all day, reminding myself of the need to think things through and make rational choices.

Right now I need to figure out who I am, because somehow I've lost myself along the way. I should be upset that he spanked me. Instead, I'm upset that he thinks I need more lessons.

I'm trying to process this. I keep replaying the situation, and my way of thinking, and demanding I look beyond the surface of what I feel. Logic. I need logic. He's trying to make sure I'm ready for the next step between us and that I won't regret my decision. Why does this upset me?

Okay. This is where I need to be honest with myself. As much as I've sworn I do not want a relationship, or the strings and heartache that go with one, this man is under my skin. I feel myself falling hard for him and looking for signs that he's falling for me, too. It's insanity. I'm a contract, a responsibility. A possession to him. He should be nothing but pleasure and the escape he has promised me he will be. And that is all he has promised.

It should be enough. It has to be enough before I allow myself back under his control, even for another encounter.

That means I need to take a few days and decide if I really can do this. I need to find myself again, the me that doesn't need anyone. The me that understands I'm the only one I have to count on in this world. The me that will allow him to pleasure me and expect nothing else in return, because expecting more from people just means heartache.

Thursday, March 17, 2011

Lunchtime . . .

I walked into the gallery this morning determined to make it about art. If anything can bring me back to me, that's it. Once

I arrived at work, though, I discovered Mark was dealing with off-site business and probably wouldn't be in all day. I felt a mixture of relief and disappointment. I know the rest of the staff is relieved when he's gone, too. He always creates a subtle tension in the air, but he also creates a raw energy that excites the entire building and the people inside, even if they don't realize it. I need that energy today.

In his absence I turned to caffeine. I was just leaving the kitchen with a full cup of coffee when Mary, my fellow sales rep, and "frenemy" as Ralph has called her, knocked into me. The contents of the cup splattered everywhere, including down the front of my—fortunately black—dress. She apologized profusely and swore it was an accident, but it wasn't. I'd thought things had improved after she'd had a meeting with Mark last week and become friendlier, but apparently her friendliness was short-lived. She simply hates me for existing and I can't control that. There is a lot I can't seem to control lately.

3:00 p.m.

*T*he gallery was scaled off to customers about an hour ago to allow the removal of the art from our personal office walls, because apparently it's part of Mark's personal collection. He must be even richer than I realized to own as impressive a collection as this one. I'd thought the pieces belonged to the gallery since his family also owns Riptide, one of the largest auction houses on the planet. Anyway, it turns out that once a year, Mark replaces the art and invites elite customers in for exclusive showings. The event is highly anticipated.

With the gallery shut for the art removal, I decided to head to the coffee shop for a caramel macchiato and was surprised to find Chris, Ava, and Georgia standing at the counter deep in conversation. Chris's longish blond hair was rumpled, as if he'd been running his hands through it while working, and there was this devastatingly sexy energy about him that, based on how enthralled they looked as he spoke, clearly had Ava and Georgia spellbound. I waited in line to order, and my attention went to Georgia. Her beauty, next to Ava's, had me feeling very ordinary. All my fears that Georgia had inspired the ring came back to me.

Chris's gaze lifted, and his brows dipped. I knew he'd seen something on my face, and thankfully it was my turn to order, which gave me an escape from his scrutiny. I have no idea what he saw in my expression—but too much, for sure. He and Mark both saw too much. But then, Chris is an artist, a man who studies details. What did I expect?

Once I placed my order and turned back to the group, I found that Chris had disappeared back to his table and Ava was attending to a customer. Georgia greeted me with such a friendly smile that it was hard to remember why I'd felt uncomfortable a few minutes before. Apparently she'd stopped in for coffee on her way to a meeting with Ralph to go over the prior night's sales and receipts.

We chatted on the short walk back and I asked her about the famous artist Georgia O'Keefe and the similarities in their work and their names. Turns out O'Keefe was her idol. Georgia had learned about their names both being Georgia (not an overly common name, she pointed out) when she'd taken an elective art class just to get the easy credit. The deeper she'd gotten into the semester, the more certain she'd been that their names were no coincidence but a sign she was meant to be an artist. Georgia's story inspired me and, for the first time in days when I walked into the gallery, I felt a sense of rightness in being there. This was where I belonged. The art, this place, was me. Is me.

That was a few minutes ago, and already the feeling has faltered. The instant I sat down behind my desk I found myself staring at the empty wall where the painting had been removed, and I knew it couldn't be just the art I love, nor could I hide behind it. Taking this job, daring to do what I'd dreamed of, had been, and is, about living life, finding myself.

And there are more parts to me, things I've only just discovered, and things I want to discover. I am still the same girl that walked in here: an art enthusiast who was waiting tables, and who dared to make my college major a career. But I am also the woman who'd stood in the coffee shop bathroom and been aroused by a spanking. I want to know all parts of me. I have to know myself to control my life and destiny. But does that mean "he" is the right man to help me make that journey?

That's what I have to decide.

9:00 p.m.

*L*ast night is repeating itself. Hot bath. Pajamas. My own bed. And again I ask, what more could a girl want? The answer is the same. Him. I clearly need to rethink my strategy, as I am in the same place as before. I feel mentally exhausted. I don't want to think about contracts, or rings, or why it hurt when that ring was given back to me, though I'm pretty sure it means that I haven't made this about sex and escape—what I vowed last night it had to be, in order to move forward with him.

Now I've been spanked, and I liked it. Not every girl can write that in her journal. And on that note, I'm going to bed and to sleep. Tomorrow I'll figure the rest out. Tomorrow it will make sense.

11:00 p.m.

So much for getting some sleep. Josh, the conservative, good-looking, safe investment banker I dated a few times, started calling me over and over right after I lay down to sleep, and he won't stop. He's drunk and out of control and I don't want to call the police, but I'm starting to think I have to. After he showed up at my work a week ago, and now this, I'm feeling very nervous about what he might do next.

I tried to bluff and threatened to call the police if he called again. He called again. I'm fighting the urge to shove things in front of my door for protection. I don't think Josh would hurt me, but I didn't think he was capable of anything he's done either, and we only dated a few times. My phone is ringing again . . .

Friday, March 18, 2011

Late afternoon, home again . . .

I don't really know where to begin writing, considering all that has happened since last night and what my plans for to-morrow night involve. But I know I want to get my thoughts down on paper so I can look back at this and know how I was feeling before it took place.

I'll start with last night, when Josh was calling me and harassing me. I don't know how it's possible, but my would-be Master and self-proclaimed keeper of my happiness and safety called right after Josh had just called me a whore and told me he was coming over. The sound of my would-be Master's voice set something off inside me, and I'd gushed out a confession about what was going on. The next thing I knew, "he" was on his way to pick me up and rescue me from Josh. I didn't need or want to be rescued, and I regretted telling him about Josh. I didn't feel ready to see him—not alone, not in his house and his bed. But there's no fighting him. He'd made a decision to pick me up and I knew he wasn't going to be stopped.

He arrived at my door fifteen minutes later, with me a nervous wreck. But when I opened the door and found him standing there in jeans and a snug-fitting T-shirt, looking casual and sexy, the power oozing off him, I wanted to wrap my arms around him. I didn't, though. I knew I couldn't touch him until he touched me. But his eyes met mine and it's like he just knew how much I needed to feel him close.

He pulled me into his arms, molding me against his hard body, and buried his face in my hair. I heard him inhale my scent and then he whispered, "I'm here."

I'm here. The simple words resonated on some deep level I needed them to. No one else was there for me in life. Only him. It scared me that I felt I needed him, when earlier I'd been so certain that I would always want more from him than he would from me. Or, maybe, more on a different level is a better definition. I know he'll push me to places I might not even think I can go, but I am almost certain I will never have the power to push him to places he wouldn't otherwise go without me. He won't ever need me. He will need power, and I think that my need for him is exactly that. His power. His power over me. Standing at my door, I told myself he was just pleasure and an escape, even safety for the evening, and I wanted to believe it, but I knew then, and I know now, that it wasn't true.

We left my apartment and had just made it to his fancy sports car when Josh showed up.

"Who the hell are you?" Josh demanded of him.

In a flash, Josh was against the car and my would-be Master said something low to him that I couldn't hear. Josh paled and then said something back before handing over his keys to "him." I stood there hugging myself, shivering from the cold night air and the intensity of the situation. More low words were exchanged, and when Josh was finally set free he apologized to me, looking like a whipped puppy, before he went to sit in his car.

My would-be Master ushered me into his warm car and, once he joined me, said, "Josh won't be bothering you again."

He wouldn't say it if he didn't mean it. "You took his keys," I commented. "How will he get home?"

"He made the choice to drink and drive. Let him figure that one out."

I couldn't argue that point.

Fifteen minutes later we entered his home, and I remember the spicy, woodsy scent—his scent—warming me all over. This place felt safe. He felt safe. It was a moment of revelation. Isn't that feeling exactly why I was able to allow him to spank me and be aroused, rather than frightened or angry? Though I'd been mad, it was about the location, not the spanking. I don't, and won't, allow my job to be affected by our relationship.

He led me to his living room, and I felt a kind of vulnerability from my need for him that I wished then, and even now, that he couldn't create in me. But I was alone with him and he was gentle in the way he'd been that night he'd come to my apartment, the night when I'd freaked out over my first reading of the contract. That felt right and good—until I saw that we weren't alone at all. The other man who'd been here before, who we'd been with, was standing by the crackling fireplace, holding a glass of wine.

"From what I hear, you need this," he said, lifting the glass to offer it to me.

My would-be Master stepped behind me, his hands sliding to my waist, his mouth lowering near my ear, "Go take the wine."

"No, I—"

"It's just a glass of wine, Rebecca," he said. "It'll calm your nerves."

It wasn't just a glass of wine, and we both knew it. It was the first step to more. Even so, after a moment of hesitation, I stepped forward, moving slowly, cautiously toward the other man. I stopped in front of him and he handed me the glass. He was as gorgeous as I remembered, tall and dark, the opposite of my would-be Master.

I'd blinked at the man whose name I did not even know, the air crackling like the fire behind him. He wanted me. I didn't want to want him, but there was this sexual tension in the room that was almost like a living creature. It was as hungry as his eyes told me he was. I knew then that if I let it happen, I would be submissive to both men. This man would be Master Two, submissive only to Master One.

I accepted the wine and sipped it, letting the bittersweet liquid slide down my throat, welcoming the numbing effect it would offer. Master Two reached down and stroked my hair behind my ear. "Beautiful," he whispered.

I don't consider myself beautiful, but the way he looked at me and the way he said it, all rough and husky, as if he meant it, made me feel as if I was. My body heated, and I remembered him touching me once before, the way his mouth had intimately licked and kissed me all over. The way his cock had thrust inside me.

Master One, the man who'd consumed me inside and out, stepped behind me again. It was him I truly responded to, his touch tingling through my body, heating my blood.

"Yes," he agreed softly, his fingers trailing down my arms, creating goose bumps on my skin. "Beautiful."

It was all I could do not to lean into him and become lost in his touch, but once I did that, once I forgot everything but him, there wouldn't be only him. There would be them—both men. It bothered me to be shared, and yet it aroused me.

I knew then that I had completely lost control of myself again. I downed the wine, and shoved the glass at Master Two before I turned to Master One. "Why did you call me tonight, when you told me to contact you when I was ready for this?"

His fingers stroked down my hair. "What's important is that I did, and you needed me."

That wasn't the answer I wanted, though I have no idea

what I had wanted him to say. Just not that. "I can take care of myself."

He laced his fingers in mine and pulled me to the couch. "Did you know," he asked, sitting down and settling me onto the cushion beside him, "that putting yourself in danger is forbidden in our contract? In fact, it's grounds for punishment."

Nerves slammed into me immediately. His spanking me had been one thing. I trusted him in ways I didn't try to understand. But I did not trust Master Two. I didn't know him. "You want to punish me again?" I asked.

His fingers wrapped around my neck and he brought my mouth to his. "Punishment is between you and me. Only you and me."

A small amount of tension eased from my body. "Then why is he here?"

"Because I want every drop of pleasure I can get from you. I want to taste it. I want to touch it." His lips brushed mine, his fingers caressing one of my breasts. "I want to feel it when your body tightens around my cock and quakes because I've fucked you so well."

My sex clenched, but I wasn't ready to cave in to passion. "And yet you want to share me." Just saying the words twisted me in knots.

He leaned back to look at me, his gaze probing mine. "When he's fucking you, and touching you, and licking you, Rebecca, I can watch every little nuance of how it affects you. It's like a window into your pleasure that allows me to not only give you more, but also be the best Master I can be. I can't do that when your hot little body is squeezing my cock into oblivion. So, let him fuck you. Let him please you. Let us give you the escape I can feel you craving."

It wasn't the answer I expected. In fact, it was everything I didn't expect, and everything I needed to hear. It was incredibly arousing—freeing, even. "Yes," I whispered, and my reward was his mouth closing on mine.

Master Two sat down behind me, his hand settling posses-sively on my hip, and this time I didn't resist him. This time I gave in to the pleasure that I knew this night could hold. They touched me, undressed me, undressed themselves. I was naked with those two gorgeous men, and they took turns kissing me, licking my nipples. Licking my clit. There wasn't a part of me they didn't touch, they didn't own.

At nearly one in the morning, I lay in bed and listened as he said good-bye to Master Two. I wondered who he was, this other Master. I wondered what came next. I'd read some BDSM sites that talked about the Master wanting the sub to sleep on the floor or at his feet. That wasn't me, and I realized just how foolish blind signing that contact had been.

The uncertainty I felt quickly brought back every one of my doubts I'd left in the living room earlier in the evening. I sat up, intending to dress, only to realize my clothes were in the other room. He appeared in the doorway then, jeans unzipped and hanging low on his lean hips, and sauntered over to me, be-fore removing them as I watched. It was hard to think with him naked, and I wondered if he knew that.

He joined me on the bed and pulled me into his arms, my back to his chest, his lips to my ear. "Get some rest. That's an order."

All thoughts of leaving faded into the bliss of being held by him. "I told you, I don't take orders well," I murmured, but the truth was that I was exhausted. "I'm pretty sure that makes me a bad candidate for your sub."

"You don't take orders well, but I like a challenge," he agreed. I almost thought I felt him smile against my hair, but he isn't much on smiling, so surely not. And there had been no smile in his voice as he'd sternly added, "Go to sleep, Rebecca."

I don't remember what came next. Apparently, I did as ordered and went to sleep.

*F*riday had become Saturday at 2:00 a.m., or that's when I remember looking at the clock next . . .

I gasped and then blinked awake to find myself alone in his bedroom, and it only took me seconds to realize I'd had one of my nightmares again. Every time I thought they were gone, they came back. I was shaking all over, and I sat up and tugged the blanket up with me, thick darkness consuming the room, feeling as icy as the San Francisco Bay water. This nightmare was different from the others, I realized. My mother wasn't actually trying to kill me this time.

Instead of being on a trolley that loses control and slams into the ocean, I was already in the water, or I wasn't really there. I was in the bay, only I wasn't in the bay. I was me, and yet I wasn't me. I know that makes no sense at all. I thought writing it down would make it more logical, but it isn't working. How do I describe what a shifting, odd nightmare is like? It was like . . . like one of those movies where someone dies and they end up watching the hospital staff try to bring them back to life from above, wherever above is. That's how this nightmare flowed. I could see myself floating face-down in the choppy waters, my dark hair spread out on the surface.

My mother was there, too, floating facedown just like me, both of us unmoving, lifeless. I figure the fact that she is already dead has some meaning; perhaps my mind is telling me I'm going to end up like her. I'm not sure if that means dead or unhappy. And I'm not sure where I was watching from. I never saw myself watching me, or rather us, but I felt the water, the ice, the emptiness. I was dead in the water, but the part of me watching was alive and I wanted to stay alive. I tried to scream and get to myself and my mother, but I couldn't make a sound. I tried to move but an invisible box confined me. I was trapped, incapable of saving myself or my mother, though it was illogical to think I could. We were already dead.

What makes a person whose dead mother was never any-thing but gentle have these kinds of violent nightmares? Uncer-tainty? Uneasiness? A sense of being out of control of my life? Isn't that what my mother always preached? Control my life, so no one else could?

These were my thoughts when "he" returned. The door opened and he entered, and I didn't care where he'd been or why he'd been gone. I just knew what had to happen. "We need to talk about the contract," I blurted out.

He flipped on the light. "Then let's talk," he agreed, saun-tering forward. He was back to wearing those sexy, low-hung jeans and nothing else. Soon he'd be naked if I didn't stop him.

I held up a hand, staying his approach. "Not here. Not in the bed. I want to get dressed and talk about our agreement for what it is: a contract. I want to go down it line by line, item by item."

He glanced at the clock. "At 2:00 a.m.?"

"Yes. Now."

Fifteen minutes later, fully dressed in the clothes we'd started this night out in, we sat at the table in a kitchen that was pretty much the size of my apartment. Oddly, his money didn't intimidate me, even though I'd never had any of my own. His money didn't attract me, either. He did.

I broke the silence. "I won't sleep on the floor or at your feet. I won't wear a collar. Ever. I know that's big in the BDSM world, but it's not me. You won't collar me."

"Fine on the floor and I don't want you at my feet. I prefer you in my bed, where I can fuck you at will. A collar is simply ownership, but to me it's more like marriage—I do not collar anyone. What's next?"

More confirmation that this is simply a short-term agreement to him. Fine, then, I was going to make sure it was very short-term. "Three months, not six."

"Six months."

"Three."

"Four, but if we decide to renew our agreement after that, I want the contract modified to include things I might want added or taken out."

"And things I might want added or taken out," I countered.

His lips curved ever so slightly. "Of course."

"I don't know what a cane or caning is, so take it out."

"Try it first."

"No. No more trying. I need to do this now or not do it at all. That's what I need you to understand. We have to come up with an agreement I can sign tonight, or there is no agreement."

"Signing before you're ready—"

"I am ready."

He stared at me far too long for my comfort before he said, "I want you, Rebecca, but once I have you, I plan to push you. I can't do that if I'm afraid you'll crumble."

"You think I can't handle this. You think I can't handle you."

"I'm not sure you think you can handle this."

I pushed to my feet and he stood up as well. "I'm out," I stated. "You're right. I can't do this—but not for the reasons you imply. I like to control my life, and I don't do well when I can't." I laughed without humor. "That sounds ridiculous, when I'm negotiating a contract to be a submissive."

"It's not ridiculous. A choice to hand over control under agreed-upon terms is not only control itself, but the freedom to let go and escape reality when you otherwise wouldn't."

"Then you have to see that lessons and uncertainty are the opposite to me. It's affecting my job and my sleep. It's making me crazy."

He stepped around the chair and pulled me close. "If you want to sign, we will, but on one condition."

"And that would be?" I held my breath, waiting for the answer.

"One last lesson. The ultimate lesson. When it's over, if you want to sign, we'll sign."

This was a test. "When?"

"Tonight. I'll pick you up at nine."

Lunchtime . . .

*H*e tried to get me to talk about my nightmares but I quickly withdrew and asked to go home. Reluctantly, he agreed. Maybe that was my test for him. I need to know he won't push me when I don't want to be pushed, and he seemed to understand this was one of those times. I can't talk to him about personal things and still make him about pleasure and escape. I'm not big on sharing my personal feelings anyway, and my mother, and the things I learned from her before her death, are as personal as it gets. I'm already struggling with my feelings for him, which give him even more power over me than any contract ever will.

He'd taken me home as I'd requested so I could try to sleep a few hours before work. I was remarkably exhausted and I'd fallen asleep almost immediately.

Even so, I was forced to stop by the coffee shop before work for a caffeine boost. Inside I found Ricco Alvarez waiting for a drink, looking aristocratic and debonair in a fitted suit. Oddly, he was in deep conversation with Mary, whom Ralph had said Ricco didn't care for. What is it about the coffee bar that was inviting meetings these days?

I ordered my drink and joined them. "Ah, Bella," Ricco purred. "Just the lady I wanted to see. Your customer dropped by my gallery and purchased several pieces. We need to do the paperwork for your commission."

My eyes went wide. "You're kidding." I was elated. When I'd taken the woman to his private showing, she'd been embarrassingly hesitant to buy. "That's such good news."

"Congratulations to you both," Mary said tightly. "I'll let

you two talk." She glanced at Ricco. "I'll bring the painting over tonight." She slipped away toward the door.

I frowned, wondering what that was about as Ricco accepted his coffee from Ava, saying something to her in Spanish before turning back to me. "Shall we go share the good news with your boss?"

I smiled. "Yes. Let's share it."

An hour later, Ricco had gone and Mark appeared in my doorway, electrifying the air as he always did. "That painting you found in Seattle—the guy sold it to me for a steal. We're going to make a fortune at auction."

I was stunned. Even now, I can't believe the sale came through. My commission is going to be . . . I can't even write down what I estimate it will be. Instinctively, I knew Mark would use my excitement for control. He plays the control card with everyone in the gallery. "That's fantastic news," I said, managing to sound cool and calm. "I can't wait to find out how well it sells."

His lips twitched. "Seems like today is your lucky day, Ms. Mason. Feel free to continue that trend. It's good for the gallery, and so, it seems, are you." He left in a whiff of spicy male wonderfulness, leaving me basking in his rare compliment.

I smiled. He was right. I'd just closed two huge sales; today was my lucky day. I just hope the night is, as well.

Sunday, March 20, 2011

After the night . . .

I wore a dress he'd sent to me by courier. Turquoise. Figure-hugging, with a zipper down the front. Expensive. My shoes were black pumps. My thigh–highs, thong, and bra were black, with sexy sheer lace. My nerves were jumping around when my doorbell rang, and I drew in a few deep breaths before I opened the door. And when I did, oh, my, he just plain stole my breath. He was scrumptious in every way.

His eyes traveled down my body, caressing it with an intimate, slow inspection, and just like that, I was wet and wanting and we hadn't even left my apartment. "Hi," I said when his gaze returned to mine, sounding like some silly infatuated schoolgirl. Feeling like one, too.

His eyes danced with amusement before he pulled me close, kissed me thoroughly, and then caressed a hand over my backside. "Hi," he replied.

When he set me free, I wobbled, and he grabbed me and held me there a moment, just staring down at me. "I've been thinking about tonight all day." His voice was rough, almost harsh with feeling.

I wet my lips and his gaze followed, sending liquid warmth to my belly and then lower. "Me, too." Just then I wondered what we were doing and where we were going. Wondered if I could pass this final test, and did I really want to? Last night, in that moment in his arms, his hard body cradling mine, the answer had come easily. Yes. I did.

"Tonight I am 'Master' to you."

"Yes." His brow lifted and I added, "Yes, Master."

Once he helped me into the sleek, silky black jacket he'd bought me, and we were in his fancy car, we rode in silence, the small space thick with sexual tension and anticipation. Our destination turned out to be a gated property in a ritzy part of San Francisco called Cow Hollow. Here the standard small houses disappear and become monstrous architectural wonders.

I knew the area but had never been there. I was basically poor growing up, with a single mom who worked in hotel sales. She did all right for us, but we weren't putting caviar on the table like the Cow Hollow crowd.

We pulled to the front of a massive concrete stairwell where men in suits, security I discovered, seemed to be waiting on us to arrive, but they didn't open our doors.

"There are rules inside that we need to cover," my Master told me, turning to face me.

"I'm listening," I said, butterflies going wild in my stomach.

"You walk behind or beside me, never in front. You speak to no one unless I tell you that you may speak. You don't even make eye contact with anyone unless I say you do."

My lips parted in shock. "What is this place?" I whispered.

"A private club that we will frequent should we ink our agreement. That makes how you behave tonight critical. You are a reflection on me here."

I nodded, uncomfortable and nervous.

"There are two sections to the club," he explained. "A public play area and private rooms for intimate play. We will be going straight to my private quarters." He studied me a moment. "Any questions?"

"No."

"No, what?" he demanded, his tone sharp, his eyes hot.

"No, Master," I replied, and I was surprised at the thrill that shot through me.

He opened his door and got out of the car. One of the security men immediately opened mine. My Master appeared and offered me his hand and I took it, letting him pull me to my feet. With my hand in his, we started up the stairs toward a set of double red doors. Two men in suits waited for us at the top, but I didn't look at them.

When we entered the house, I stepped onto an expensive Oriental rug and immediately felt as if I was in the movie *Gone with the Wind,* the room was so elegant. An extravagant chandelier hung overhead and a winding, red-carpeted stairway twisted and turned toward an upper level.

My Master motioned me toward the staircase but he didn't touch me. We made it halfway up when a striking man in a dark suit headed down toward us.

"Head down," my Master ordered a moment before we paused for him to greet the newcomer.

"And who is this?" the man asked.

"My lovely new prospect," my Master replied.

"Indeed. May I admire her?"

My Master touched my back. "Look at him," he ordered.

Admire me? I fought the urge to back away and somehow I lifted my gaze to stare into the man's eyes, my heart thundering wildly in my chest.

Raw male interest flashed in his stare. "Innocence personified," he murmured, cutting his attention to my Master. "Will you be taking her to the main floor?"

"No. I'll be keeping her to myself."

Relief washed over me. The man glanced back down at me. "A pity." He gave me a small bow. "I hope to see you again soon." He stepped around us and I let out a breath.

"Come," my Master said, urging me up the stairs and leading me to another pair of red double doors.

We stepped inside a small sitting room with high-backed chairs. A separate door led to someplace, I didn't know where. My adrenaline was cranking up so hard and fast that the soft sound of him locking the doors behind made me jump.

He stepped behind me. "Untie your coat."

I did as he ordered, and I heard the quiet whisper of the cloth as he disposed of it. My Master stepped in front of me, and looking into his eyes, seeing the possessiveness in them, shook me to the core. I could barely swallow, let alone think.

"This," he said softly, "is the only room in my private quarters where you are allowed to wear clothing. Undress, Rebecca."

I drew a slow breath, nervous to undress without knowing what was behind the other door, but I knew that if I was going to do this, to let him be my Master, I had to trust him. I unzipped the dress and let it fall to the ground.

"All of it," he ordered.

I stripped off my panties and bra.

"All of it," he repeated.

I kicked off my shoes and then peeled away my hose. When I finished, his gaze swept over my body, his expression fiercely primal. I craved his touch and hungered for him to undress. He gave me neither of these things. Instead, he hit a button on a remote I didn't realize he'd been holding and the mystery door slid open. He stepped aside and motioned me forward. "Stop just inside the room."

Anticipation burned inside me as I walked toward the door and tentatively entered. Beneath my bare toes, a thick, luxurious burgundy carpet absorbed my steps. Candles flick-ered, creating a sweet vanilla scent in the huge circular room. There were two more doors, one on each side of the room, and a wide archway directly across from me. A large chaise longue sat by one door. A small pedestal sat by another. Drapes were positioned at several places on the walls and I wondered what they covered.

But what really caught my eye was the archway that I couldn't see beyond. My Master stepped behind me, leaning in close but not touching me. "Go through the archway, Rebecca."

For some reason, I knew whatever was beyond that arch would change me in some way. I knew that no one would ever use the word "innocent" when talking about me again. A part of me hesitated, holding on to that innocence. Ignorance can be bliss, the truth painful. My mother had taught me that all too well. But not knowing the truth, the facts—I don't want that ever again.

With that thought, I walked steadily forward. I wanted knowledge. I wanted to know whatever there was to know. I didn't want to be naive and blind anymore about anything if I could help it.

I walked up three stairs to the main level. Curtains covered every wall around a circular room that was empty but for a ped-estal in the middle that held some sort of steel archway shaped like the one I'd just passed through.

"Stand in the center of it," my Master ordered.

I moved forward without hesitation. I'd come that far and I wanted to complete what I'd started. Once I stopped under the archway, he stepped in front of me. "On your knees."

I did as he commanded.

"Hands behind your back and lace your fingers," he ordered next. "Don't move them or I'll bind them."

Again, I did what he ordered, the position thrusting my breasts high in the air. His hot stare swept over them, puckering my already sensitive nipples, and I could almost taste his hunger, his desire. He enjoyed me bowing down to him. I know this as I write, as surely as I knew it in that room. He enjoyed the control it gave him. The power. And I was aroused by those things in him, wet and slick between my thighs.

"I can choose to let others watch us in this room," he informed me.

My heart jackhammered and I opened my mouth to object when he added, "But tonight we just observe. You observe and discover all that you don't know." He hit a button on the remote he held, and the curtain behind him began to lift to reveal a gigantic video screen.

My Master moved to stand behind me, allowing me to see the image of a man chained to an archway like the one around me, two women on their knees before him, licking him and teasing him. "He's being punished, Rebecca," my Master explained. "The female on the left is his Master."

Punished? The man seemed to be enjoying himself, his expression stark with desire, his hips thrusting forward. I was certain he was about to come. Abruptly, though, the two women pulled away from him and began kissing each other, leaving him wanting for completion.

"Each time he nears release, they stop," my Master explained. "It's a far worse punishment than flogging or whipping."

The channel changed and a new scene appeared. A woman stood on a pedestal on top of a stage, tied to another archway with what must have been twenty-five people surrounding her. A man dressed in leather used a whip on her back and she bucked against each blow. I could see pain etched in her face. I watched the whip come down on her and I gasped with the impact I imagined she felt. I couldn't watch it again. I needed to get out of there. That woman needed out of there.

I dropped my hands and started to get up. My Master wrapped his arms around me and pulled my back to his chest, burying his face in my hair. "Stay. I need you to stay."

He needed me. Those words were probably the only ones that could have penetrated my need to escape. As they seeped into my mind, my body relaxed against his. But my mind was uneasy—fearful, even. "Is that what you want to do to me?"

"I told you I wouldn't ever punish you in public, and I won't. This is about seeing everything that goes on here, so you aren't shocked later."

"Somehow I think I will still end up shocked later."

He didn't deny that I was right. Instead, he stood up and walked around to squat in front of me, his finger sliding under my chin. "We decide what we do. We make our rules. And you always, and I mean always, have your safe word. Say it now, Rebecca."

Looking into his eyes, I felt myself coming back to him, calming fully. "Red," I whispered.

"Red," he repeated. "You know it. I know it. I'll listen when you use it. I'll stop whatever I'm doing, no matter where we are. The control is ultimately yours." He hit the remote on those words and the curtain closed, but not before I saw the woman grimace with another blow that set me on edge again.

I hugged myself, suddenly aware of my nakedness. "She was being beaten."

"When I spanked you, were you aroused, Rebecca?"

"I didn't expect to be."

"But you were."

I squeezed my eyes shut without answering.

"Answer, Rebecca," he ordered, his voice hard, sharp.

"Yes."

"Look at me."

I forced my eyes open. "She is also aroused," he insisted. "Her Master isn't taking her anywhere that she doesn't want to go. It's his job to know her like no one else does, like I want to know you. And showing you these things tonight helps us both know what you want and where your limits are, in a way that just reading a contract didn't allow. Unless you've decided you want me to take you home."

He wanted to know my limits. Once again, he'd said the right thing at the right moment. "No. I want to stay. I want to continue. What next?" I swallowed hard. "Master."

His eyes flashed with approval. "You will stand up, and I will tie you to the archway so you know what being in the center of this room, the showcase of the scene, and at my mercy, is like."

I was okay with his mercy. Maybe he hadn't earned that, but it was an instinctive feeling I had with him or I wouldn't have been there at all. I pushed to my feet. He stood before me, staring down at me for eternal seconds before he ordered, "Raise your right arm to your side." I did as commanded and he bound my wrist to the archway with some sort of rubbery cuff that didn't bite into my skin, then repeated the action with the other arm.

He stepped back, as if he was the audience that might be behind the curtain. I knew what he was doing; forcing me to feel what being on display would be like. With my arms wide, my body naked, his eyes hot as they caressed every inch of me, I have never felt so exposed in my life, but neither have I ever been so aroused.

Time ticked by eternally, and finally, he began to undress. I was spellbound by his male beauty, his long, lean, athletic body. His cock was thick and hard for me. He wanted me. He was turned on by my being tied up like this. My gaze tracked his path as he moved to my right and I watched him open a cabinet with rows of whips, chains, and various toys inside, and my heart raced. He ran his fingers over one item, then the next, and I knew he meant to taunt me, to build anticipation and make me wonder what he intended to do to me.

His selections turned out to be a flogger with long leather tassels and a flat leather crop. I let out a hot breath of relief. I didn't know what a crop would be like, but I knew what a flogging felt like, and I'd enjoyed it. Familiar territory in unfamiliar surroundings was welcome.

With his toys in hand, he approached me, all sleek muscle, with a predatory gleam in his eyes, before he stepped behind me. His cock pressed beneath my backside, his breath whispered on my neck.

"You were relieved I picked the flogger."

"Yes."

His hand came down on my backside and I jumped at the surprise, the erotic contact. "Yes what?" he demanded.

"Yes, Master," I panted.

"I chose it because I knew you wanted me to. Because it's my job to know what you want. What is your safe word?"

"Red," I answered.

"Say it again."

"Red."

"Use it and I stop. Understand?"

"Yes, Master."

He began to massage my backside. Anticipation burned inside me. I knew the first blow would come soon but not from which toy, and my sex clenched and ached. My nipples tightened. His hand left my body and I sensed him take a step back. I held my breath and waited to discover if the flogger or the crop would come first. The first light smack of flat leather sent a spike of adrenaline through me. A series of repeated smacks to my backside immediately followed. None of them hurt, but my skin heated and I became so wet and needy that my thighs clenched against the emptiness I needed filled.

Without warning the long leather tassels of the flogger splayed over my backside, heavier than the crop, sending waves of sensation through me. A motion of leather on skin repeated over and over, and the room faded, and all ability to think began to disappear. It was heaven, freedom from worry, from the outside world. From the need to control anything at all. I gave in to the sensations. I wanted my mind to become a blank canvas. I craved more of the prickling pain that morphed moments later to pleasure. And he gave me more, using the crop in short, gentle pats on my breasts, between my thighs, and on my legs.

I barely remember the moment he dropped the crop and the flogger and untied my wrists. I only know that I was suddenly weak, exhausted both physically and emotionally. I collapsed against him and he lifted me, carrying me from the room. I curled into him, his warm body my cocoon, and I didn't even question where he was taking me. I'd given myself to him some time back under that archway.

Our destination turned out to be a bedroom off the main room, where dim lights cast a glow on the massive bed. I melted into the velvety-soft blanket beneath me and rolled to my side, off my sore back and backside. My Master slid into bed behind me, and began to kiss every single place he'd used the leather on. He was gentle, worshipping my body, kissing me, telling me how beautiful I was. How perfect I'd been under the archway. Amazingly, time had, once again, stood still, and the sting of the leather faded. I was lost in my Master, in the way he commanded my body. Yes. In that bed, I knew him as Master more than I ever had, and I understood the escape that came from giving him that control, and the pleasure he promised would come with it. At some point I faded off to sleep, into a blissful, sated state of wonder.

• • •

I woke up this morning in his private chambers, with him wrapped around me, holding me. I remember so very clearly the moment I inhaled the luxurious male scent of him, absorbing the delicious weight of him pressed to me. And I remember blinking in surprise as the velvet box came into focus on the blanket in front of me, open to display the ring. My throat tightened at the sight and I sat up, the blanket falling to my waist, displaying my naked body.

My Master raised up on one arm and leaned in to lick my nipple, the intimate act sending ripples of pleasure through my aching, satisfied body. "Now or never," he challenged me with a hot, intense stare. "Isn't that what you said yesterday?"

I had, and there was no hesitation in my reply. Not after the way he'd made love to me the night before and known exactly what I needed, what I craved. "Now" I reached for the ring, sliding it onto my finger.

He leaned down and kissed it. "And now," he said, possessiveness in his tone, "you belong to me."

I belong to him. Despite his saying this to me before, the ring, the finality of our agreement, hit me with a bit of a shock. I belonged to someone else?

"Say it, Rebecca."

I blinked at the order and realized that this was the real test—not last night. This was the moment I would give him my ultimate trust. It was terrifying. I'd only given that kind of complete trust to my mother, and she'd betrayed me in the end.

But I'd taken a leap of faith when I'd taken the job at the gallery, and it had paid off.

I was in too deep with him now not to take a leap with him. But I prayed then—and I pray now—that he deserves it.

I drew in a breath and breathed out the words that gave him all that power over me. "I belong to you."

Rebecca's Lost Journals Vol. 4:
My Master

Journal number . . . ?

(It's been so long since I wrote, I don't remember),

Entry number 1

Friday, May 4, 2012

7:00 a.m.

I woke up with tears streaming down my face, lost in a dream, unsure where I was . . . a dream, or was it a nightmare? How can anything "he" is in be a nightmare? But how can it not be, if I'm this tormented in its aftermath?

I was standing naked in my Master's private chambers, in a room filled with red and white roses. They were everywhere, the scent of them sweet and seductive, the smell of romance and passion. My skin was ivory perfection, more beautiful than I ever remembered it being. My hair was dark silk that flowed down my shoulders. I didn't feel like Rebecca Mason. I felt like someone else. Someone compelling and enchantingly sexy.

He entered the room, standing before me fully clothed. It was part of his power, him being dressed. Me being naked. I liked his power. It excited me. It made me burn. To be possessed by such a man, this man, was everything I wanted, everything I craved.

He held out his hand. "It's time."

Nervous excitement shot through me. Yes. I will be his. And then, suddenly I was at the door of a large room with an octagonal stage. There were theater-like seats filled with rows of people. I felt a sudden surge of panic, a need to turn and run away.

"I've never claimed anyone as mine publicly," he said softly, stroking my hair. "Only you."

A knot formed in my chest and my belly. This was his way of showing me commitment; maybe the only way he knew how to show it. He was claiming me and asking for my acceptance into this community, and both things meant something to him. I had to do this for him, no matter how uncomfortable it made me feel.

He stepped forward, heading down the aisle leading to the stage, and I knew to follow, to keep my head down. I was his submissive, his slave, and he was a respected Master among what he considered his peers. I understood the dynamics, even if they weren't easy for me to navigate—not in public. Not during any of the times when he involved other people in our time together.

I was glad to have my head down, relieved not to have to see the eyes I felt like heavy, wet blankets on my skin. I didn't want these people to see me. I didn't want them to want me, yet I felt the lust and hunger of those watching me, clawing at me, suffocating me.

Once I was on the stage he turned me to face him, his hands sliding to my face, his eyes finding mine. "Do you know how proud I am of you? How perfect you are?"

The rest of the room faded away. There was only him, and the moment he turned me to the crowd and announced me as his. He then pressed on my shoulders and I knew to kneel down, lowering my head, my hands outstretched, palms flat on the floor as he'd taught me. A long line of people began to line up to come to the stage and, one by one, they touched my hair, my back, my arms. I could feel myself shake, and not from arousal. He was sharing me again, and it shook me to the core, no matter what the reason, no matter what the rules specific to this club said, that this was part of my being accepted publicly. I tried to fight the shivers running through me, but I couldn't. I slid into a dark place in my mind but it wasn't shelter enough. Every touch of a stranger's hand sent another shiver down my spine, and my eyes burned until tears streaked my cheeks.

And that's when I woke up, crying as I had been in my sleep, the scent of roses teasing my nostrils (so very real, though it was imaginary), my gaze sweeping his bedroom, where I'd been sleeping with him for months now. It took a moment to realize where I was, and why I was alone. He was out of town and would be until Tuesday. "He" being my lover, my Master, and, I fear, soon my heartache. The bed was empty without him, the house emptier, but clearly my dreams and my thoughts were not. They were rich with a growing sense of unease.

I'm in the living room now, his living room, a cup of piping-hot coffee beside me, and the television is on, but my efforts to stop my mind from racing aren't working. Now, for the first time in months, I'm forcing myself to do more than jot down random thoughts here or there as has become my habit, or rather lack of one. I'm going to start writing down what I feel again, and face what is bothering me.

And I know there is plenty bothering me. The nightmares of my mother trying to kill me have been back for a month, but now I've apparently decided to keep things interesting and have nightmares about the man I love. Who doesn't love me.

There it is. No more analysis needed. One journal entry, and I've solved the mystery that isn't a mystery.

He. Doesn't. Love. Me.

It's that simple, and yet it's complicated in so many ways, starting with the fact that I know he cares about me in the way he believes is the ultimate showing of affection and commitment. He simply doesn't believe in love. He believes in belonging, in ownership . . . in contracts. I've often thought that he trusts what is in ink more than he trusts what is in his heart or mine.

I can understand this. I can. Let's face it, my mother loved me, but she lied to me. She lied in ways that I believe affected the very core of who I am.

Looking back now, I think the security of a contract was part of what drew me to our arrangement. I know he has something in his past that makes him need that security, too, though he tells me this lifestyle is nothing more than who he is and what he enjoys. There is more in the depths of his eyes, though, more to who he is. I'd thought I'd discover what that is, who he is. I thought we could heal together. I thought we'd find love together—but he says love is a facade that twists people in knots, and yes, he's gone so far as to say that it destroys.

He's wrong. Love isn't a facade, but yes, it does twist you in knots. And he is completely wrong about love destroying what it touches. It's people who do that. And I fear that is where this is headed for me.

The scenes we enact together take me deeper and deeper into the places I know represent his internal hell, and yet I can't pull him back. Instead, he's pulling me inside that dark hole that is his escape. Only there is no escape for me anymore: not when every scene pushes me beyond the limits that mean pleasure for me. He doesn't see that, either. And as my Master, he should.

Oddly, as I'm beginning to find me again, I think he's completely lost me. Or maybe I've lost him. My heart just contracted at this conclusion. I love him. Why did I let myself love him?

10:15 a.m. . . .

*H*e called me as soon as I sat down at my desk.

"My bed needs you in it."

I swallowed hard at his raspy, desire-laden words. "It had me in it. You were the one who wasn't in it."

"Any bed I'm in needs you in it. You should be here."

"We both know why I never travel with you."

"Yes. And we are going to talk about that at the contract renewal."

I wasn't going to agree to go public with our relationship. I already battled people thinking I was too young to have depth to my knowledge. Having them believe I got where I'm at because I'm involved with someone connected to the gallery would be even worse. "My position won't change."

"We both know I can be very persuasive."

Yes. We both knew that all too well.

He lowered his voice, roughened it up in that way he did that made me insanely aroused. "I can't wait to have you beneath me again. I'll call you later."

"Yes. Later."

We hung up and I sat there, twisted in those love knots, before grabbing my journal to write this entry, to explain what I am feeling so I can look back at it later and make informed decisions, not emotional ones. Tormented. Confused. Uncertain. Out of control. Those are the feelings that have been dictating my actions, rather than logic. Which is exactly why I need to be writing this.

*R*alph just poked his head into my office and held up a piece of paper that said "61 days," his score card of the number of days my fellow sales rep Mary has been nice to everyone. It's a record, and I suspect it has to do with the fact that she discovered a couple of pieces of very special art that Mark bought for a steal for the July Riptide auction. Of course, she hates that I'm coordinating the auction, but I think she finally feels like she is on solid ground at the gallery again. Thank you, is all I can say. Give her a big commission and keep her happy. Her meanness to me this past year has been the shark in the gorgeous water that is the gallery for me.

I laughed at Ralph's antics, as he intended me to. I love

Ralph, I really do, but I don't let myself get too close to him. He wants to know too much about my private life, and that isn't going to happen.

I'd stopped writing at work because I was worried about someone finding one of my journals. It's why I don't use names. It would be bad enough to have my innermost personal thoughts exposed, but worse to expose someone else's secrets through my writing. And this time I bought a journal with a lock attached to the cover. No one needs to read my thoughts, not even "him."

I can just imagine if Ralph found one of my journals. Okay, leave it to Ralph to make me smile again, because thinking about the look on his face (he's quite prudish) if he read just one of the erotic scenes I've described since heading on my submissive journey makes me want to laugh. I might wound our quirky, sweet little accountant for life.

Yes. My life outside this place is definitely not for anyone else's consumption. I started a friendship with Georgia O'Nay that I pulled away from for the same reason. She was too close to people I know, too close to the things that would allow her to know my secret lover. But it turned out she knows anyway, for no reason I could control. The truth is, there are several people who know, and fighting public knowledge is probably a lost cause. This bothers me. It really does.

Eventually it's going to come out that I am with him. Eventually every bit of success I've had will be questioned. If I believed in where he and I were headed, it would be okay. I'd deal with it. But I guess that's what it really comes down to. I don't believe in where we are headed.

Maybe . . . maybe I need to leave the gallery, to find another job in art—but wouldn't I still be in the same circle of people? And I'll never make the money that I make with Riptide, and I'm alone, with no one else to count on.

Yes, I have him.

But for how long?

8:00 p.m.

An hour before closing . . .

I've decided I need to go home to my apartment tonight. I'm not looking forward to telling my Master that. We're at contract negotiation time again and I know he'll freak out and think I'm pulling away from him. Maybe I just won't tell him. He won't know; he's off in another state right now.

I'll decide later. I just need some space of my own. Of course, all of the things I use daily are at his place. I'll have to go by there, and I wish I didn't. When I smell his scent, see his things . . . it's hard to turn away, but I feel like that is where this is headed. I need more than another contract, and less of what he'll want included in the new one, anyway.

I just don't think he can give those things to me.

11:00 p.m.

My apartment. It's so very strange to be here, but nice. A whole lot more humble than my Master's elaborate place, but I like that. This is me, with my overstuffed, overused couches and my down comforter on my full-sized bed, which I'm sitting on now with all my old journals surrounding me. It's a cozy little place, made cozier by it being mine, something I claim ownership of. He tried to pay my rent as part of our last contract, but I refused. I needed to know I had my sacred place I could go to if I ever needed to, and tonight I did.

Though I've made some money from the auctions and I can afford to get a bigger, fancier place, I'm not going to. The Riptide auctions that I'm involved with are only a couple of times a year, and I want a nest egg before I start spending outside my norm. I've done way too much throwing caution to the wind this past year. I might splurge on a few pieces of art and decorate a little, though. Make it even cozier.

Yes. I think I will. This idea pleases me, yet it makes my stomach burn. I'm thinking about leaving his place. I'm thinking about needing mine.

For now, though, I just packed enough of my things for the weekend and went grocery shopping. He called while I was at the store and he knew something was wrong. He told me he did. I told him I was exhausted. And I am. Emotionally. I'm on an emotional rollercoaster ride and he's not. That bothers me. It's telling. But what is it telling me?

I told him I'd call when I got home, before going to bed. I have to call him. He is my Master. At least for two more weeks.

The call . . .

*Y*ou aren't at the house," he said the instant he answered, not bothering with "hello."

My heart jackhammered and I didn't ask how he knew. Probably the security system. I should have thought of that. "No." I hesitated. "I'm at my apartment."

The line crackled with electricity. "Why?"

"You aren't there. I have no reason to be."

"I want you there. That's reason enough."

It used to be enough. And it could be again, so very easily, if he'd just . . . what? I don't even know. "It's almost contract renewal time. I wanted some space to think through what that means to me."

"What does that mean, Rebecca?"

My chest hurt. "I'll let you know when I figure it out."

"Figure it out at home."

"This is home for me."

"No. Home is with me."

He was wrong. It was his house. His couch. His everything. "And you aren't there this weekend, so home is here."

"You belong to me," he reminded me softly. "You belong in my bed. I need you there."

I could hear the rough quality to his voice and I knew he was upset. I knew he didn't want to lose me. But I also heard the word choices he always makes oh-so-cautiously. I belong to him. Not with him. I belong in his bed, not by his side—or in his life.

I drew in a deep breath and let it out. "And I need this weekend here. Please, Master, grant me this. Just while you are away." I knew the use of "Master" away from our play would help my cause, and it did.

There was silence, and time ticked slowly by, but when he

spoke he granted my wish. "When I return, I'm going to make sure you never want to leave again."

"I don't want to leave," I whispered.

He was silent again, even longer than before. "I'll call you in the morning."

"Okay."

We both sat there, and I knew he didn't want to hang up any more than I did. We do have a bond. He does want me. I know this.

"Goodnight, Rebecca," he finally said, his voice low, sandpaper rough.

My throat thickened with emotion. "Good night," I replied, and added because I had a burning desire to please him, "Master."

Saturday, May 5, 2012

1:00 a.m.

My bed surrounded by my old journals

*I*t all comes back to the roses . . .

The roses in the dream (or nightmare) have been bothering me all day. The day my Master introduced me to the club, there had been no roses. My mind had to be telling me something, and I think that is part of why I wanted to be here tonight. I needed to clear my head of everything that is my Master, and get inside my thoughts.

So I started reading my own writing. The old entries are

eye-opening, especially since I've lost track of my feelings these past few months, sporadically at best scribbling notes in random places when, and if, I have the privacy to do so. I told myself it was because I didn't want my Master reading about my feelings, but I think I just went through a period of denial. I didn't want to see everything in my life clearly as I had wanted to in the past.

One of those random entries from back in January made me pause for all kinds of reasons. It's the entry that made me begin this entry with "It all comes back to the roses." I'd written it the night before our last contract renewal (which we've continued every four months). I'd still been in my apartment as often as I was at his house, but he'd wanted that to change.

I'd been afraid of losing complete control of me. To escape into a "scene" with him, or even a weekend of being his submissive, was one thing. To live it day and night felt like quite another.

And so he'd done what he always does: He found a way to seduce me into doing what he wanted. He sent me roses; twelve dozen in different colors. They were gorgeous buds that hadn't blossomed yet. The card is what had really gotten to me, though. It read: "They are delicate and ready to bloom, like you are, little one."

It had started with a scene.

I remember the two nights before the roses so very clearly. Those two nights that had led to his sending them to me.

Night one had been at the club.

I was in the center of the playroom (that's what he called the round room in his private quarters) on my knees, my hands bound behind my back, my spine erect as he'd instructed, my breasts thrust high in the air. He stood above me, naked and powerfully male. I was aroused; passionately, intensely aroused. I could feel him in every inch of my body. It was amazing how easily he drew me into a whirlwind of lust and need where nothing else existed. It is this overwhelming feeling that is addictive, the escape from the rest of the world. The submergence of reality in a cloud of hot sensuality.

He walked to stand in front of me, staring down at me, his long lashes low over his eyes, a flogger in his hand. "It's time to play a new game."

A moment of nerves rippled through me. I never know where he'll take me, only that he's slowly been pushing me to darker and more intense places, places I go to please him, even when they frighten me.

He used the tassels of the flogger to tease my nipples in a gentle flicker over one and then the other. They tightened into hard little knots and I was aroused. He bent down in front of me and tugged them with his fingers, watching my face as he did. I moaned and my lashes fluttered.

He brushed his lips over mine. "You are so beautiful when you're aroused. I want to show you off to the world." His tongue snaked out to lick against mine again. "I'm going to open the curtain and show you off."

I stiffened. "No, Master. Please." He kissed me again.

"You can do this."

And I had. I'd done it though I hadn't wanted to, yet somehow it had aroused me. It was one of the first times I'd been truly scared of what was happening to me. There have been many more in the past few months, since our games have become different . . . darker. So much darker. But that was the first time.

Or maybe the first time was with Master Two. Yes. I was freaked out then, too; confused by how aroused I'd been by his sharing me when I'd also felt so unimportant because he'd wanted to share me. I'm always confused by Master's need to share me. And more and more, he seems to need to. Is that his way of avoiding intimacy? Avoiding allowing us to go to those places I want to go?

After the scene, he'd known I was upset. He'd taken me to his bed and kissed me from head to toe, in that way he does that always pulls me deep under his spell.

*N*ight two had been a dinner date at Louie's, a restaurant we'd both come to love and with a private room and entrance; there is no fear of our relationship going public. Sharing things we enjoy, like food and conversation about the art we both love, always makes me feel more like we are a real couple. And yes, Master/sub is a real couple for some, a deeply committed and intimate relationship. For us, I felt like it was his wall to keep us from being more. Still, I broke through that at times, on nights like these, when we enjoyed meals. Not that all of our tastes are quite the same in food, but I've done my fair share of luring him to Oreo and French fry land, as much as he's lured me to finer dining.

The waiter took away our plates. "Your normal desserts?"

"Two crème brûlées," Master confirmed. "A caramel macchiato for the lady and plain coffee for me."

The waiter bowed his head and departed, pulling the private door closed behind him. I sighed with satisfaction. These moments when we simply relaxed, when we weren't on the edge of something intense, were too few and too far between.

"You seem content," he said, studying me.

"I enjoy this place."

His eyes had warmed. "I'm glad you do." He had reached inside his jacket and pulled out several folded sheets of paper. "It's time to renew our contract. I thought we'd go over the details."

Renewing our contract is a topic of mixed emotions for me. I'd hoped we'd be more than this by now, and the confirmation that we are not tightened my belly. "You want changes?"

"I want you to agree we stop hiding in a closet."

"No. I can't do that. That would affect my career."

He studied me a long moment. "What if I said I want you to move in with me?"

Hope filled me. "Move in with you?"

His voice lowered. "You're the only sub I've ever asked to do this."

The only sub—I'm still in that box. So living with him was just another way of controlling me. In fact, it was his way of controlling me around the clock, instead of only during the weekends that our last contract had dictated I be his.

"I'll pay your rent for the contract term," he added. "Then

you have the security of knowing that if we don't renew again, you have a place to go."

"No," I said immediately and stood up. It was clear I was never going to be to him what he was to me, and I just wanted to go home.

He was on his feet in an instant, pulling me close. "Why?" The waiter came in and my Master gave him a sharp look that sent him into retreat. Once the door shut, he stared down at me. "Why, Rebecca?"

Why didn't matter. It changed nothing.

"Please take me home, and consider anything you start tonight, or for the next two weeks, to come with the word 'red' on repeat." I'd never used my safe word before but I was using it then. I didn't want to be under his control. Not then, and maybe not ever again.

"Rebecca." He leaned in to kiss me.

"Red," I hissed. He hesitated and I added, "You said you would stop whatever you were doing if I used it."

His jaw flexed and flexed again, but he pulled back. "I'll take you home."

"Thank you," I whispered.

The trip to my apartment was short but felt eternal, the silence unbearably thick. He parked in the lot behind my building and killed the engine. We sat there in the darkness. "Why?" he asked again.

Was that all he could do? Ask me why? I gave him so much of me, and he couldn't even tell me how he felt about my refusal?

I reached for the door. He caught my arm. I cut him a hard look and said, "Re—"

He cut me off with his mouth, shoving his fingers into my

hair and slanting his mouth over mine, kissing me, claiming me in a way he'd never done before.

I tried to resist him, but I tasted more than need in him. I tasted his fear of losing me.

I barely remember how, but suddenly his seatback was down and I was on top of him, forgetting that I was in my apartment parking lot. In seconds he was inside me and I was riding him, grinding my hips against his, reveling in him filling me, touching me. In the way he couldn't seem to get enough of me.

When I finally collapsed on top of him, I lay there and listened to his heartbeat, fighting a wave of emotion very unlike me.

"Move in with me, Rebecca," he ordered softly.

"Why?" I asked this time.

"Because I want more than we have now."

"But not the same kind of 'more' that I want," I whispered. "And I'm not sure how I let that happen."

He slid his hands to my face and forced my gaze to his. "It's the only kind of 'more' I know how to give."

"Maybe that isn't enough for me."

"How do you know if you don't try?"

"I just . . . do."

"You are more to me than any other sub has—"

"Don't," I said, rolling off him and struggling into my seat. "Don't finish that sentence!" By the time I was sitting where I belonged again, he'd raised his seatback.

"You're upset. We'll talk about this tomorrow."

"No." I managed to awkwardly deal with the mess we'd made of my clothing and my emotions. "I don't want to talk tomorrow. I

want to go to work and love my job and not think about this at all."
I got out of the car and he followed. I knew he would. The Master
must protect—right? But who was going to protect me from him?

At my apartment, I turned to him. "Goodnight." I opened
the door to go inside.

He gently shackled my arm. "We'll talk tomorrow."

"I'm done. This isn't me. It never was."

His eyes glinted hard. "I'm going to change your mind."

I didn't answer and he let me go.

I quickly went inside, before I did something stupid like
telling him to change it right now. I rested against the other
side of the door and I could feel him doing the same on the
outside.

He is an addiction, and addictions are never good for you.
He's taking me deeper into his world, deeper into his dark de-
sires, but I'm never able to get behind the physical aspect of our
relationship. I just lose more of who I am.

*A*nd then came the roses . . .

They arrived at my door the next morning, and I was se-
duced by the romantic gesture. And later, when we talked, he
assured me that these new, darker places I could feel him taking
us was just another part of discovering us, and delving into a
deeper level of trust.

I was scared. I knew it meant that calling him "Master" would
take on a new meaning. But I convinced myself that if I wanted
more from him, maybe he still needed more from me first.

And so I gave up what was left of my life outside of being

his. I thought I wanted my life to be his life but somehow, by letting him control more of me, he gave me less of him. The things I have done to please him . . . well, let's just say I'd never do them for anyone else. I've gone everywhere he's asked me to go. I've gone places I never thought I could go. Done things that shredded me inside and out. Now, I need more from him.

9:30 a.m.

At my desk . . .

I have work to do, important details for a big event we are hosting off-site Sunday night. A local artist who paints food is showing at a new bakery owned by the renowned chef Michael Adams. I set up the event after a visit to the bakery, managing to arrange for the chef and the artist to attend. It's like nothing the gallery has ever hosted, and Mark actually complimented me. Even after all of this time, a compliment from "Bossman," as Ralph calls him, is hard to get. But then, he put me in charge of the Riptide auctions. I'd say that is a pretty big compliment.

And I should be thinking about the event, calling customers to confirm they are attending, rather than focusing on the fact that "he" hasn't called me, and what that means. I should go get coffee and clear my head. Yes. I'm going to get coffee, and not next door. I'm sticking to the kitchen and the gallery.

3:00 p.m.

*C*ontrol. He has it. I do not. I want it back. He thinks I already have it back, and now he's punishing me for it. He still hasn't called me. He's reminding me that he has the power to make me need him, to crave the sound of his voice. And I do. Damn it, I do. I never doubted his power over me, though I keep reminding myself that his actions say he is doubting it. He's the one trying to prove something that I already know: I need him. And he's worried that I don't. That has to mean something. Staying at my apartment has been the smart thing to do. And I'm off tomorrow, with lots of time to myself to think. It's not only given me space to think but also spawned some in him. Maybe, just maybe, it can be a catalyst for something different for us.

Oh, God. Amanda just told me I have company. Master Two is here, claiming he wants to talk about a painting I've been helping him with. But I know that's not why he's here.

10:00 p.m.

My apartment

I'm on my couch with a pizza box open on my coffee table. I ate half of a large cheese, plus one extra slice. And some double-stuffed Oreos, though I mostly licked the cream out of them. Funny how stress makes me eat one minute and the opposite the next. Apparently tonight was "feed the problem" night. Does the fact that it was all junk food have any meaning? Oh, yeah. You betcha.

But now that I am stuffed, I have no more excuses left for not writing this entry. Tonight it is clear to me why I've withdrawn from my writing in my journals. Creating the entries really does force me to face feelings I'd rather not face. The same reason I've ignored my Master's calls. I'm not ready to face where things are going, or not going, between us.

So, let's see. Where should I start writing? This afternoon, which I consider the beginning of the end with my Master. I need to think of the event I'm about to describe that way. I need to remember that this relationship I am in is not the one I want, nor is it what I ever set out to develop. I have to remember this when I see my Master again.

No, when I see "him" again—when I ensure he is no longer my Master. Because today was unacceptable. Today was the final straw that broke the camel's back, as my mother would have said.

Master Two came into my office, dressed in a suit and looking his usual handsome, debonair self, his eyes hot with an intent that told me I was right to be worried. The laptop in his hand, free of a case, was the next indicator.

He shut the door. I stood up, my spine stiffening. "We don't meet when he's not here." My heart was thundering like a hard, heavy drum and I thought it might break my breastbone.

"He wants me here," he assured me, stalking forward, and coming behind the desk before flipping open the screen and watching the system boot up. He hit a few keys and began to dial up a video program that I knew better than I wanted to.

Master Two stared down at me with so much primal heat, I cut my gaze to the computer. "He" appeared on the screen and my thundering heart sputtered a moment. "You know how I feel about my job and personal life being mixed," I hissed at Master.

"This does nothing to hurt your job," Master assured me. "You are simply meeting with a legitimate customer."

Master Two wrapped an arm around me and pulled me against his hard body. "I'll make sure no one suspects anything but business happened when I leave." His hand glided over my backside and he turned to pull me flush to him, letting me feel his hard cock against my stomach.

"No," I panted at him and, damn it, I was aroused. My body (or maybe it's my mind) is programmed by my Master, with the help of Master Two (far too often for my happiness), to react automatically to them.

But I was at work, and that had me clinging to sanity. My fingers dug into his arms. "Not here. Later. When I'm home."

"Right now," Master said softly. "Here. Do it because it pleases me." He paused. "Or don't. This is your decision. It's always your decision."

I hated how aroused I was, how easily I could say "yes" and forget the important barrier I'd put in place. And once I forgot it, he'd forget it. I'd be headed down a path I didn't want to go. In some corner of my mind, I knew that's how I'd ended up here. I had let myself go places just to please him, places I wasn't comfortable going that led to darker and darker places.

Master Two leaned in and whispered in my ear. "I'd like to set you down in that chair, spread you wide, and lick you into oblivion. Just say the word."

I squeezed my eyes shut and my thighs together. This was part of the power play. This was my Master proving to me he still had this kind of power over me. Or maybe he was proving it to himself.

I fought to remember the journal entries, and the reasons

why I should or shouldn't do this. He needed this. He needed to feel he still had this hold on me. Didn't loving him mean giving that to him?

"Yes," I whispered. "Yes. Okay."

Master Two yanked my slim-cut teal dress to my hips and turned me so that my backside was on display for my Master. I could feel his hot stare on my body and my skin heated, my breasts growing heavy, my thighs tight. Master Two cupped my backside and squeezed, his eyes finding mine, his breath warm as it tickled my lips.

"It's all about you, baby. Moan for me. That's all I want." He turned me and set me in the chair and before I could blink, he was on his knees in front of me, spreading my legs. But then the roses flashed in my mind. I'd thought giving him more meant he'd give me more. Maybe . . . maybe I needed to give him less.

"Red," I said, murmuring my safe word. And then louder. "Red."

Master Two immediately dropped his hands from my legs. I stood up and pulled my dress down and turned to the computer screen, shaking. "I can't do this. Not anymore."

I saw a flash of something in his eyes that I want to believe was pain. Knowing we are falling apart is destroying me, and I need to know he feels something, too. I gave him the power to hurt me, and I gave him my heart. He never promised me his. He never promised me anything he didn't give me.

The computer screen went dead and I had to walk Master Two out, making small talk and pretending that his hands had not just been on my backside, that my thighs were not slick from how near his tongue had been to licking me.

When I returned to my desk, my cell phone immediately rang and I knew it was my Master.

I didn't answer. I can't talk to him. And it's not even because I'm angry. It's because I'm weak. I'm always so damn weak with him.

Midnight

*L*ast thought of the night. No more contracts. No more being shoved into a box of his design. I'm still willing to go where we've been, and be submissive during erotic play, but not at other times. Not on his terms only.

Tomorrow, when I see him, we will be different. I will be different. I'll be me again, the woman he wanted when all of this started.

Okay, a second last thought that seems unrelated—or maybe it's not. Maybe it's just an indicator of how much of a wreck I am right now, but that weird foreboding I had for weeks last year is back. I hate the feeling, the sense that something terrible is going to happen. I just keep telling myself nothing terrible happened last year. And nothing terrible is going to happen now.

Sunday, May 6, 2012

8:00 a.m.

I'm sitting in the coffee shop next to the gallery, at the same corner table that I once sat at when my Master charged in, took me into the bathroom, and spanked me. That memory is why I'm here—to remind myself that I drew a line in the sand that day. It's part, though not all, of the reason I rarely come here anymore.

Ava is the other part, and not just because she saw us come out of that bathroom together. Ava is . . . I think I'll save her for another entry. I have enough to fret about as it is.

Back to that day here in the coffee shop. When my Master, who wasn't my Master yet, had spanked me in the bathroom, it had aroused me and confused me. Just thinking about that moment when he'd yanked my skirt up and made me agree to let him spank me, and the moment his hand had touched my backside, the erotic charge that had followed, sent a sizzle down my spine. And when it was over, the easy way his fingers slid inside me had shattered me into orgasm. I'm wet just thinking about it, when I should be angry. Exactly what I felt then.

Regardless of liking what he'd done to me, I hadn't liked where he'd done it. I'd set a hard limit of nothing between us ever happening at a place that was frequented by those involved with the gallery.

It was the only hard limit I've ever set, though there were other limits I'd liked to have set. The only one—and yet he crossed that line yesterday. He knew how I felt about this when he sent Master Two to me yesterday. I need to remember that, in order to stay strong.

I am not just a way for him to feel powerful. I won't be that anymore.

11:00 p.m.

The event was spectacular. The desserts a little piece of heaven. I passed on the crème brûlée; I couldn't get myself to eat his favorite sweet. The artist, a kindred spirit with the name of Rebecca Knight, sold several paintings and was beyond ecstatic. And now I'm at home, about to take a hot bath, alone.

"He" didn't call. He hasn't called again. And he won't. That would give me the power. And lord only knows, that would be a sin. I'm just glad I'm off tomorrow. I plan to organize my apartment and do a little decorating.

Monday, May 7, 2012

7:00 p.m.

*L*ast night, or I guess technically early this Monday morning, around twoish, there was a knock on my door. I sat up with my heart thundering, flashing back of the night Josh had gotten drunk and threatened me, then showed up at my apartment. I still can't believe a guy I dated a few times went quite so crazy, and I still can't shake the feeling he's still around. Maybe that's the foreboding feeling?

I'd wrapped myself in a robe to cover my skimpy "PINK" sleep shirt and stood at my door. "Who's there?"

"It's me, Rebecca."

His voice slid through me like hot buttered rum, warm, rich, and enticing. The weakness I'd feared he would evoke in me was instantaneous, and I hadn't even opened the door. I pressed my hand to the wood separating us. "You aren't supposed to be back yet."

"Are you going to let me in?"

I thought of saying "no," but it wasn't a real consideration.

I had to see him. I had to feel him close. I turned the lock and pulled open the door.

He stood there, so damn devastatingly handsome, his hair and clothes rumpled like he'd had a rough night of travel. And the look on his face did me in. His eyes were dark, tormented, his expression stark, worried, expressive. He thought I might turn him away, and it was eating him alive.

At that moment, I didn't care why he worried or what his motivation might be. I didn't think about the impact of a Master as powerful as him losing control of his submissive, and how it might make him react. All I knew right then was that he was afraid of losing me. And me him . . .

We moved at the same time. I backed into the apartment and he stepped inside, kicking the door shut. I was in his arms in a flash, him lifting me, my legs wrapping around his waist. His mouth came down on mine and he tasted like more of that hot buttered rum I'd heard in his voice, but better, spicier. Sweeter, because I'd feared I'd never taste him again, or feel him, or touch him.

He laid me down on my bed, coming down on top of me, and our lips parted, breaking the drugging kiss. He stared down at me, his eyes intense, stormy.

"How are you here?" I whispered, daring to touch his cheek without permission, reveling in the way he let me.

"I had to see you." His mouth came down on mine again, his tongue stroking deeply, possessively. And yes, there was a command in the kiss, a command that I submit, but there was more, too. There was passion, so much passion. The kind of passion he holds in check and denies me.

He wasn't in check then. He wasn't in control. But neither

was I. Not with his big, wonderful body on top of mine, the weight of him arousing me, teasing me with the moment he would be inside me. I wanted that so badly, it hurt.

He tugged my robe loose and his hand slid over my ribs and caressed my breast, fingers teasing my nipple. A moan slid from my lips, and he swallowed it with another long, sultry stroke of his tongue. I was sinking into the oblivion Master Two had promised me in my office but had never have come close to providing. Only "he" could really take me there.

I tugged at his shirt, needing to feel skin against skin. He pulled it over his head and tossed it aside, displaying rippling muscle from the waist up. "Take your shirt off," he ordered, standing up to finish undressing.

Yes, get it off and get him back on top of me, where he belonged! I'd barely tossed it away when he was back on top of me, his hands on my breasts, mouth on my neck. I arched into him, trembling with my need for him, this man who has called to me in a way no other human being ever has or perhaps ever will again.

He was thick between my slick thighs and my fingers dug into his shoulders, but I couldn't pull him closer. I wanted him closer. I wanted him inside me. His mouth was traveling down my neck, over my shoulders, back up again. These are the moments that I revel in, when he doesn't hold back, when he doesn't restrain me or himself. We are just . . . us. We are just lost and alive and passionate. They are few and far between, and this was one of those times—and more. We kissed each other like we were breathing life into our bodies, like we couldn't survive without each other. I'd never felt this with him, never felt as if he needed me as much as I needed him.

Finally he parted my legs and slid between them, hovering above me, his eyes connecting with mine, and I felt him everywhere, clear to my soul. I know. I know. That sounds a little crazy and like I'm romanticizing the moment, but I'm not. I felt him everywhere.

He pressed inside me, stretched me, and sank deep, until we were one, joined together, and I had this sudden moment of fear it might be the last time. Something flickered in his eyes and I almost thought he felt it, too, and that it shredded him as much as it did me.

With a low guttural sound, his mouth came down on mine harder, his kiss darker, more commanding, as if he could stop whatever might follow this if he claimed me then. He dragged his cock backward along my sensitive flesh, and then he thrust hard. I gasped as sensations rocked from my sex through my body.

It was a wild frenzy of us trying to get closer, to get him deeper, to get more, more, more, and more. More what? I don't know. Just more. It's the only way I can describe how it felt, and I loved how NOT controlled it was, how not in control he was. LOVED. IT.

When it was over, we collapsed together in a hot, sweaty wonderful moment of satisfaction that became several minutes. Slowly, our breathing became less labored, our muscles relaxing, bodies melting into each other's. Neither of us spoke. It was as if we both thought words would destroy what our bodies had communicated.

At some point, he grabbed a tissue from the nightstand and gave it to me. When I would have gotten up to go to the bathroom, he pulled me back against him, wrapping his leg over mine and burying his head in my neck. I had the impression he thought that if I left the bed, I wouldn't come back.

Looking back now, he might have been right. My mind would have started running as wildly as my body had just responded to him, telling me all the reasons why what I'd just done had been a mistake.

"Let's sleep," he said softly.

No command. No demand that we go to his place.

"You're going to stay here?"

"Yes. I'm staying here."

Stunned, I lay there a moment before a smile curved my lips and my lashes lowered. He was here. And he was willing to do things he wouldn't normally do.

It was enough for the moment.

And then the nightmare came . . .

I was floating in the icy bay facedown again, alone. So cold and so alone. Everything went black and icy and then black again . . . and then I was above my body, watching it float.

In a heavy gasp for air, I sat up, shaking from the impact of the dream.

He was there, sitting up with me, his strong arms wrapping around me from behind. "Easy, baby. You're okay. It was a bad dream."

I sucked in a hard-earned breath and tried to bring the

room into focus, the tension in my body slowly easing. He stroked my hair, reminding me he had gentleness in him and that it had been a long time since he'd let me see it.

"You haven't had a nightmare in months," he murmured.

"They've come back," I whispered and let him pull me back down so that we were on our sides facing each other. He grabbed the blanket from the foot of the bed and pulled it over us. I rested my head on my pillow and he did the same on the spare beside me. Had we ever lain face to face like this in bed before?

"What time is it?" I asked, since the clock was behind me.

"Five."

"No wonder I'm still tired."

"You're off today. You can sleep. Tell me about the night-mare."

"I can't." How did I tell him what I didn't understand? And I didn't want to, anyway. The nightmares are like my journals. Sacred and for my knowledge and viewing only. "If I do I won't get any rest."

He didn't push me, like he usually does. He simply took my hand, pulled it between us, and covered it. "Then sleep," he said again, and this time I heard the familiar command in his voice.

I went to sleep. I suspect maybe we both thought it was because he ordered me to, but later, we both realized the truth. He'd already lost his control over me.

The next time I woke up, sunlight pierced my sleep-heavy eyes, and the bed was empty where he'd been. I was alone, just like I had been in the water. Any distress I felt over "his" absence faded into a replay of the nightmare, the sensation of floating facedown in icy water making me shiver.

An overwhelming urge to go to my mother's grave washed over me. I had to go. Today. This morning. My chest tightened painfully and my guilt twisted in my gut. I hadn't been to see my mother in a year. I just . . . I don't like to think about her betrayal.

"Coffee?"

His voice startled me and I sat up, the blanket falling to my waist. He was in my doorway, shirtless, in only his boxers, and rippling with sculpted muscles. His gaze swept over my breasts and I tugged the blanket up to cover myself. That drew an arched brow from him.

I'm sure it did. It's not like modesty has been at the forefront our relationship. Scratch that, and correction: our agreement. But he was in my home, and what I wanted from him had changed.

Okay, scratch that again. What I wanted hadn't changed; I'd wanted more than a contract from the beginning. I just wasn't willing to settle for less anymore.

I arched a brow back at him. "You made coffee?"

"I make coffee at my place."

He did, but something about his doing it at mine didn't fit his Master image, though I can't say why.

He sauntered forward, muscles flexing, and he was the most delicious breakfast a girl could ask for. The mattress shifted as he joined me and offered me the cup. "I added your favorite creamer."

He did those things for me. Bought the creamer I liked. Stocked my favorite bubble bath. But then, Masters cared for their subs' needs, often in a quite sexy, sensational way. For us, though, I felt more like a child and he was the parent.

I sipped the hot beverage without taking my eyes off him. "Thank you," I murmured, wondering about the way he was silently studying me. He was giving off a weird vibe. Uneasiness? Was he nervous? No. Surely not. Not him.

We stared at each other and neither of us spoke, an indicator that we both knew we were at a crossroads. We frequently talked politics, art, and whatever else came to mind, but we didn't talk about us. About what we were, or could be, or would never be—and that was what was in the air. That was the crossroads.

"Come home," he said, breaking the silence.

"You mean go with you to your home."

"We live there together."

But he didn't call it my home. "This is my home. Your home is where I stay when our contract indicates I do so."

"This apartment is merely a backup—"

"No. This is my home and it's going to stay that way." I suddenly wanted to get away from him, but the hot coffee made a fast departure impossible. It also made covering my naked body impossible. And I wanted to be covered. "I'm going to go shower. Can you please let me have some privacy?"

A flicker of hard steel flashed in his eyes before he took the cup from me and set it on the table. Before I could blink, he'd stalked to my side of the bed, scooped me up, and was carrying me to the bathroom. He set me down, turned on the water, and then wrapped me in his strong arms. "You want to shower, you can shower with me."

He didn't give me time to think, dragging me behind the curtain. And, damn it, I was weak. I did a whole lot more than shower with him. That man had me pressed against the tile wall and his cock buried deep inside me before the water was even hot. The sex had been hot.

*A*n hour later, dressed in jeans and a gallery T-shirt, with tall black boots, my dark hair brushed to a shiny mass, I was determined to be stronger. I walked into the living room to find him facing away from me on the couch, watching the news. He was so determined to stay with me that he'd grabbed his suitcase from his car and changed into clean clothes. I knew he was determined to do whatever he had to do to get me back to his proverbial castle where I'd be his submissive.

He twisted around, clearly sensing my presence.

"I need to run out for a while," I told him before he could speak.

"I'll go with you," he said, pushing to his feet to face me.

My lips parted in surprise at how far he was taking this. "It's nothing you'll enjoy."

He narrowed his eyes. "Is it important to you?"

"Yes."

"Then it's important to me."

I didn't take these as encouraging words to indicate he wanted more depth to our relationship. A Master made his submissive's needs top priority—some of them, anyway, I had learned. He was simply trying to figure out where he gained control again.

For an instant I considered telling him "no," but the need to go to my mother's grave was growing more insistent. If I let myself get into a confrontation with him, my time to visit her could slip away from me. "Okay."

His eyes lit with victory. "I'll drive."

Of course he would. He hated the practical used car I'd insisted on buying myself, when he'd wanted to buy me something fancy. Besides, even if I had a fancy car, the passenger seat just wasn't the place for a Master.

*T*he drive to the town of Colma on the northern end of the peninsula is a short ten miles. It's a quaint little place with only two thousand residents, and I'd like it, if not for the fact that it has seventeen cemeteries and about five million dead people. Even though I'm not superstitious, it bothers me. There is nothing that steals your control more than death, and death loves Colma.

"He" knew where Colma was when I told him our destination, and I was thankful that he didn't ask questions. It fit our pattern. We don't talk about our families, aside from the basics like who was alive and who was dead. So he knew I was visiting my mother. Or her grave. My mother was no longer anywhere I could visit her.

He parked near the grave and I didn't wait on him to get out of the car. I tugged my jacket around me and started walking through the cold, breezy cemetery, feeling as if there was a concrete block strapped to each of my lungs, crushing them inside my chest cavity. He fell into step with me, and right then, seeing him as my Master and protector didn't seem all that bad.

When I got to the tombstone, a simple white square with my mother's name on it, I stood there, unable to stop the memories from playing in my head.

"How could you not tell me?"

She'd straightened in her hospital bed. "How did your knowing help anything?"

"You thought letting me think that he simply didn't want me was better than letting me know who and what he was?"

"He was involved with dangerous things I didn't want you involved in. He still is."

"I want his name."

"No. I will not die knowing he might drag you to the grave with me."

I squeezed my eyes shut, guilt assailing me. She'd been dying, and I'd confronted her with anger. But what was I to do? She'd smoked and taken horrible care of herself. She was dying and leaving me, and still she wanted to deny me my only other family member? The bite of more memories, of her dying, of the casket, of the pain, overcame me. One after another, I re-lived the moments that had left me alone in this world.

"Are you okay?"

I blinked to realize I was on my knees and "he" was actually there with me. How had I ended up on the ground? "Yes." I pushed to my feet and he helped me. "I'm okay. I'm done here."

"Is your father here, too? Do you want to visit him?"

I'd told him I didn't know my father, but "he" had not lis-tened.

That hurt. It hurt badly, reminding me how alone I am. "He's not here," I bit out. And apparently my Master had never been "here," as in fully present in our relationship, either. I charged toward the car.

Once we were on the road, I thought of how bitter my

mother was about men. How much I now think my father affected everything she was and everything she became. Maybe she's warning me from the grave that I am headed there, floating in the dark, miserable waters of my own creation. Or maybe it's just my mind using her as a tool to warn me of the same.

He drove us to some oceanside café, and the instant he placed the car in park, I turned to face him. "I won't sign another contract. If you want to see me, ask me on a date."

He just sat there, unmoving as stone, his expression an emotionless mask, until finally, he said, "You know that isn't how I operate."

My stomach clenched and I faced forward. "Yes. I know."

More silence. More unbearable silence. "Why don't we go inside and talk about the contract?"

"No. I don't want to talk about it. I want to go home." I cut him a look. "To my apartment. *My* home."

His eyes narrowed; his jaw clenched. He looked like he might refuse, but he put the car in gear and backed away.

At my apartment, he walked me to my door. I turned to face him. "Thanks for . . . everything."

"I'm coming inside."

I shook my head. "I need to be alone." And it was the truth. It was time I learned how to embrace taking care of myself again.

"We can make the contract work."

I opened my door and stepped inside before facing him again. "I don't want to make it work."

He grabbed me and pulled me to him, kissing me with

wild, sultry passion before setting me back from him. "This isn't over," he said, and turned and walked away.

I shut my door and leaned against it, hugging myself as I slid slowly to the floor. I had never wanted him to be right more than I did now.

I didn't want "us" to be over, and yet somehow, I found myself reaching down and sliding the delicate rose-shaped ring he'd given me from my finger. I could no longer be his unless he was truly mine. And he isn't. I'm not sure he ever will be.

The Master Undone: An Inside Out Novella

While *Rebecca's Lost Journals* can be read in any order, if you plan to read the rest of the Inside Out series, *The Master Undone* should be read after *Being Me* to avoid a major spoiler. The reading order would be *If I Were You, Being Me, The Master Undone, Revealing Us*. If you don't plan to read the rest of the series, please read on now and enjoy!

Lisa Renee Jones

One

—

"Another scotch and soda, Mr. Compton?"

On any other day I'd stop at one drink—but not today. I hand the flight attendant my empty glass. "Leave out the soda this time."

"You got it," the woman says, smiling brightly. "Scotch straight up, on its way."

Her overly cheery tone hits a raw nerve, reminding me of just how fake much of the past two years of my life has been. But then, I let it become that way. I chose to ignore things I shouldn't have, and someone I cared deeply for paid the price.

As if that isn't enough, I'm rushing to see my mother through her unexpected cancer diagnosis and emergency surgery. There's nothing fake about that. It's as goddamn real as it gets.

Loosening my tie, I sink down into the deep first-class seat, attempting to get comfortable despite feeling shredded. I'm hoping a little more alcohol will give me some much-needed sleep between San Francisco and New York, and maybe slow down the demolition process going on in my mind.

Yeah. That would be good. Anything to stop my mind from running wild. I'm supposed to be able to control my thoughts. I'm a *Master*. A title that defines who I am and how I stay grounded. My thumb is always on the pulse of everything that happens around me—or so I thought. For the first time since college, I'm not sure if that's true. I'm not sure it was ever true, and I don't know where that leaves me. I don't know who that makes me.

"Scotch straight up."

Inhaling a heavy breath, I turn back to the attendant and accept the drink. "Thank you." My gaze touches her badge and I add, "Ms. Phillips."

"Call me Emily," she encourages, and her tone is far warmer as she asks, "Is there *anything* else I can get you?" There's no mistaking her flirty, lingering emphasis and I study her, taking in her attractive features in a completely removed fashion. She is pretty, a brunette, which I favor, and well-endowed in all the right places, but she is not what I need. And I *do* need. Sex is my drug, not booze, but it's no escape right now. Not when I don't have control. Never without control.

I down my scotch and hand my glass to Ms. Phillips.

She arches a delicate brow. "Another?"

"Not this time. I know my limits." And I value my minimal control too damn much to give any more of it away to a bottle of scotch.

Ms. Phillips's lips curve seductively. "I bet you do," she purrs. "I'll be around if you need me." She walks away.

Turning back to the window, I assure myself that I *do* know my limits. What got me in trouble was forgetting my rules, getting too close to my sub when I knew she wanted more than I had to offer. Silently, I curse. I can't bring myself to think of the woman I've lost as just that—just a sub—but I struggle with the emotions her name stirs inside me. And I have to stop struggling. I have to get control of myself.

Rebecca. There it is. Her name. And with it, her eternal absence that I can never mend. The news of what became of her is still too raw, only forty-eight hours old. I'm struggling to deal with how my mistake led her into the path of another jealous woman with a horrific outcome. This is twice in my life I've let someone get close to me, only to see that person hurt. I'll never let that happen again.

Never.

Once my flight lands in New York, I'm anxious to get to the hospital. I quickly make my way to the baggage claim and locate my carousel. With some fast footwork I'm at the front of the crowd and I've just snatched my single piece of luggage, besides the one hung over my shoulder, when I hear, "Mr. Compton?"

I turn to find a pretty blonde standing before me, her long, silky hair draping the shoulders of her pale pink, primly cut suit jacket. I arch a brow at her. "And you would be?"

"You are *the* Mark Compton, correct?"

"I'm Mark Compton," I confirm, wondering where this is headed.

"I thought so. I recognize you from your picture at Riptide." Her perfect pale cheeks flush. "Oh. Sorry. I should introduce myself." She offers me her hand. "Crystal Smith, the new head of sales for Riptide, and thrilled to be working at one of the most prestigious auction houses in the world."

I don't reach for her hand. But my need to avoid touching her isn't control, it's weakness—and I hate weakness. I close my hand over hers. "Nice to meet you, Ms. Smith." My palm warms, and I don't want to be warmed by this woman, or by any woman I haven't chosen as a submissive.

Her lashes lower, and I know she's hiding her reaction to the touch. Despite myself, I am intrigued. Even more so when, almost instantly, she smoothly recovers and her lashes lift, her eyes directly meeting mine. Any sign of whatever she'd felt is gone.

Impressed by her rapid recovery and quick control, I'm surprised by how reluctantly I release her hand. I'm rarely reluctant about anything. "Since when is it the duty of the sales manager to pick someone up at the airport?"

Her brows dip and she gives a delicate snort. "It's not like you're just anyone. You're your mother's son."

I inwardly cringe at the sore spot she's hit. I love my mother, but there's a reason why I opened my gallery across the country. "She ordered you to pick me up."

Her lips curve. "Your mother's as feisty as ever from her hospital bed."

"I'm not surprised," I manage tightly. Just thinking of my mother in a hospital bed creates a dull throb in my gut. "She's impossible to say no to, even for me."

"I thought for sure her pride and joy would be the one person who could."

Fighting a wave of something dark I'd rather not name, I struggle to maintain my normal steely composure. "My mother is the only person I *can't* say no to."

She gives me an odd, quizzical look. "The only person?"

"Yes, Ms. Smith. The only person."

She frowns. "I'm sorry," she says, and then waves me toward the door. "My car's parked in a fifteen-minute spot. We'd better run before I get towed." She turns and starts walking, expecting me to follow.

I stare after her. She's *sorry*? What the hell does that even mean, and why do I have this intense need to race after her and ask, when I never run after anyone?

Two

—

I catch up to Ms. Smith at the sliding doors, where a cold gust of October air blasts us.

She shivers and hugs herself. "I guess I shouldn't have left my coat in the car." She flicks me an amused look. "And I guess you're too macho to need one?" She doesn't wait for my reply, waving me forward yet again and declaring, "I'm freezing. Come on!" She takes off, running across the walkway to the parking garage.

For a moment I just stand there, watching this curvy, petite Barbie doll race away from me *again*. An irritated sound escapes my lips and I scrub my hand over my twelve-hour stubble before caving to the inevitable beginning of my pursuit. *Chasing her.* Again. I'm chasing this woman I barely know, who is supposed to be my employee.

I cross the roadway and fall into step with her. "I'm right there," she says the instant she sees me, pointing at a black Mercedes.

Interesting. I assume the car means she's done well at Riptide, though I'm not sure how she'd have had time to see the benefits. I don't remember her at all from my most recent visit last month. Either way, her success is exactly what I want. It feeds more success, and the last thing I need right now, with my mother incapacitated, is a sales manager who doesn't know how to close a deal.

Ms. Smith heads to the driver's door and I follow, holding out my hand. "I'll drive."

She gives me a look like I'm insane. "*You* want to drive *my* car?"

"Yes."

She frowns. "No."

Surprised, I reply, "I'm driving, Ms. Smith." My tone is non-negotiable, and I'm damned good at nonnegotiable.

But she isn't rattled. Her brows dip and she actually begins to negotiate with me. "If I agree to this, then you have to agree to stop calling me 'Ms. Smith.'" She makes quotation marks with her fingers. "That's what people call my mother."

I almost laugh. This woman is a piece of work. "You really don't care that I'm temporarily your boss, do you?"

"Being my boss doesn't allow you to drive my car, and I would think you'd want to call me by a name that makes me feel relaxed. I'm in sales. Feeling all edgy and nervous gives me performance anxiety."

My lips quirk at her logic and her boldness. "And my calling you Ms. Smith makes you edgy and nervous?"

She studies me a moment and there's this odd look on her face, like she's somehow reading something I haven't said. "I feel nothing you can't solve by calling me Crystal." She pauses and adds, "*Mark*." The obvious challenge loses steam as she visibly shivers and makes a frustrated sound. "Fine. You drive." She clicks the locks open, then dares to grab my hand and presses the keys into my palm. "I'm too cold to stand out here and debate name usage."

She starts to pull away, and my instinct to automatically take control kicks in. I grab her hand, and her lips part in surprise, her gaze colliding with mine. Heat flares instantly between us, defying my certainty that this woman is absolutely not for me, twisting my gut in knots at the poor timing of such an attraction. There's a hint of some unidentifiable emotion in her eyes that I try to read, but she cuts her gaze away, clearly attempting to block my efforts.

"Don't wreck my car," she warns, looking at me again.

"I won't wreck your car," I assure her and pause for effect, as she had, before adding, "*Crystal.*"

She smiles and my gaze is drawn to her mouth. Her lips are full, sensual. Kissable. They're as interesting as she is, though I have no business finding anyone interesting anytime in the near future.

"Thank you," she replies, mimicking my pause before again saying, "*Mark.*" She tugs on her hand and I let it go. With a dash, she goes around the trunk to the other side of the car.

I shake my head and, as impossible as it seems, I smile. My mood is remarkably lighter as I place my bags in the backseat and then slide into the car myself. She's a refreshing glass of water when I'm drowning in hell, and, damn it, she smells good, too. A scent I can't place, but it makes me think of the hot buttered rum my mother makes at the holidays.

"I guess you're a control freak like your mother?" Crystal observes as I start the ignition.

I shake my head at her boldness again and glance at her. "Do you filter what you say at all?"

"Filtering makes other people filter, and then you never get to know them. I prefer to know who I'm dealing with."

"As do I," I agree. "I just approach things with a bit more subtlety."

"Ohhh," she laughs. "Is that it? I lack subtlety?"

I put the car in gear and back up before flicking her a look. "You're direct."

"I guess you could say I like directness probably as much as you like control."

"In ten minutes you think you have me figured out?" I challenge.

"In ten minutes you think you have *me* figured out?" she counters.

I pull into to the payment line and cut her a sideways glance. "Who said I was trying?"

"Right." Her lips twitch. "Of course you aren't."

"Spare me the effort," I say. "Tell me about yourself."

She shrugs. "Like what?"

"Where's your family? Do you have siblings?"

"My family is here and I have two brothers, both of whom work for the family business."

"Which is what?"

"My parents own Arial."

I barely contain my surprise. "The monster technology company?"

"That's right."

I'm instantly concerned. No wonder she's fearless. She doesn't have to work or make a sale. Her family is why she has a Mercedes.

Has my mother's illness caused her to make rash staffing decisions? I discard that idea. She just found out about her cancer a few days ago. I hope. Has she known longer and not told me? Is the cancer worse than she's let on?

". . . and I really like it," Crystal says. "What about you?"

I shake off my thoughts. "Sorry. You like what?"

"I've lived here my whole life. I love New York. How about you?"

"I grew up here," I reply absently. "Why exactly are you working for us and not Arial?"

"Aside from technology boring me to no end, I don't want to ride my family's coattails. I need my own life and my own achievements. And I need to do something I love. I love art and Riptide. And I love your mother. If ever there was a woman who can rule in a male-dominated world, it's her."

There was a quality sure to impress my mother. A woman set to make the world hers, not his, whoever he might be. Exactly what I don't like, and everything she does like. "How long have you been at Riptide?"

"Three weeks."

Which explains why I didn't meet her on my last trip. "Tell me about those three weeks."

We spend the rest of the drive talking about Riptide and her impressive coordination of the upcoming auction. I absorb myself in what she's saying, and by the time we pull into the hospital garage, Crystal has successfully distracted me from thinking about the dreaded moment when I see my mother and face the reality I've never wanted to face: she's not indestructible. It hits me now like a block of ice, and I feel frozen to the soul.

I turn off the car and the lights slowly dim. Darkness settles around us, but I don't move. Silence fills the car before Crystal softly says, "She'll be okay," and her palm lightly settles on my shoulder, a warmth spreading through my body that I cannot fight, any more than I can bring myself to remove her hand. I let her touch me. I never let *anyone* touch me.

I grunt. "Right. Because she won't have it any other way." I mean it to come out a joke, but it comes out as grim as I feel. I open the door, not sure why I've let this woman I barely know see emotions I try never to feel, let alone allow anyone to experience with me.

Almost instantly she's by my side, with an oversized purse half her size on her shoulder. I guess her to be all of five feet two, minus the four-inch heels she manages with practiced ease. "What hotel are you in?" she asks, smartly dropping the topic of my mother.

"The Omni off Madison."

"Good choice," she approves. "Close to Riptide and out of the Times Square crush."

She astounds me. Not only do I not ask for people's approval, they usually don't offer it voluntarily. But for reasons I don't understand, I don't tell her so. I just don't seem to have it in me to care who's on top right now.

*W*hen I enter the hospital room, I find my mother sitting up in the bed with her back to me, arguing with my father. "You give his arm too much credit. He needs the cool calm that Mark had on the mound to be a real player."

The reference to a past I don't want to remember, or announce to Crystal, makes me quickly change the topic. "Are you telling Dad how to run his ball team again, Mom?"

My mother turns around, her long blond hair bouncing with the curls she meticulously creates each morning, her blue eyes lighting on me. "Mark!" She holds her arms open and I go to her, sitting on the bed to wrap her in a hug. Over her shoulder, my gaze meets my father's worried one. His light brown hair is rumpled and strain is etched in his features, the lines framing his steely gray eyes deeper than they were a month ago. He's shaken, which shakes me, but I don't show it. They need me to be the rock I've always been.

My mother pulls back to inspect me, as she always does. She looks good, still ten years younger than her fifty-five years, and as strikingly beautiful as ever. How can she have cancer? How can she be in this bed?

"And for your information, son," she scolds, "I'm looking out for your father. I want him to get the seven division championships in a row he hopes for, and he won't get it with his present pitcher." She turns to my father. "Steven, I insist you show Mark the practice tapes. He'll see what I mean."

"You know I'd like it if Mark watched the playbacks, Dana," my father agrees, and I feel him watching me, even though I don't look at him. "He just doesn't enjoy watching them with me."

"I love baseball," Crystal chimes in, walking to a chair to sit down, and saving me from a topic I don't want to address. "One of my brothers played in college and I never missed a game." She glances at my father. "I've wanted to go to one of your games ever since Dana told me you coached."

"You can join me in the box seats when the season starts," my mother tells Crystal. "I planned on offering anyway."

Crystal's face lights up with excitement. "I'd love that."

My mother smiles and turns her attention to me, rumpling my hair with her fingers. "You look a mess. Your tie is half off and you have bags under your eyes."

My smile is genuine, if strained by worry. "Leave it to you, Mother, to tell me exactly how it is. It's been a long day, but worth it to get here to see you." That ache in my gut throbs, and I again think how crazy it is that she looks this good when she has stage 3 breast cancer. I soften my voice. "How are you?"

I watch emotions shift on her face. Uncertainty. Worry. Fear. And finally, "I'm pissed." Her voice cracks. "I don't have time for cancer, and . . ." She abruptly looks around me at Crystal. "Did you bring those reports I wanted?"

"No," I say firmly. "You're not working the night before you have a double—"

"Don't say it," she hisses. "Don't say it. I can't . . . just don't." She turns to my father. "Steven, I need some water, please."

My father quickly hands her the cup and I sit there, frozen in place from seeing my strong, unbreakable mother struggling for composure.

"I forgot the reports in my trunk," Crystal says, popping to her feet. "My trunk sticks. Mark, can you please come help me?"

My mother spits her water out and almost chokes on a sudden burst of laughter. "Mark?" she inquires, glancing at me. "You let her call you Mark?" Her gaze flicks to Crystal. "I knew I liked this girl. She knows how to put a man in his place. No 'Mr. Compton' for her."

My eyes meet Crystal's, and when I expect her to gloat, she gives me an apologetic look. "Would you help me? Please?"

I give her a nod. I need a minute to get a grip on what

I'm feeling, anyway. Something I never feel or need—but I do now.

Following her into the hall, I pull the door to the room shut.

The instant I turn to face her, she confronts me in a soft whisper. "I thought you couldn't say no to your mother. Why would you start tonight, when she asked for the reports?"

I'm taken aback and irritated. "You barely know any of us. Don't try to tell me how to handle my mother."

Her lips tighten and her eyes meet mine, and suddenly her expression changes, as if something in mine has softened her. Which is impossible. I'm unreadable. She surprises me by taking my hand in hers. I surprise myself by letting her.

"You're trying to protect her," she says. "I get that, but she's having a double mastectomy, Mark. She wouldn't even let you say the words. She needs work to keep from thinking about it."

I stare down into her pale blue eyes, and I don't know what's happening to me. I don't have control. She has control. Worse, she's right about my mother.

I trust this woman more than I trust myself right now. And that scares me in a way I haven't been scared in a very long time.

Three

—

At nine o'clock, a hint from my father to leave them alone sends me on my way, and I head to the lobby. To my surprise I find Crystal, who I thought had left a good hour earlier, sitting in a waiting room chair with her laptop open. She doesn't notice me and I find myself watching her work. I'm drawn to this woman, who's the complete opposite of my type, for reasons I don't understand. Maybe it's simply that she's different from everything familiar, and everything familiar feels wrong right now.

Her brow knits adorably as she keys some kind of data into whatever program she has open, long strands of her blonde hair draping her shoulders and cheeks. My groin tightens with an image of that hair draped over my stomach and hips, and guilt twists inside me.

It's too soon. I only just discovered that Rebecca's absence hadn't meant she was traveling the world with the rich businessman she'd met. It meant she was gone forever.

And I remind myself that Rebecca was the one person who saw beneath my mask. She knew what I've always known: that sex is a tool for me. It's how I survive, how I block things out. How I blocked *her* out. I was always honest with her. I never promised her love. But, damn it to hell, I selfishly convinced her to try to live without it. Maybe with her, I came as close to love as I'm capable of ever coming. I did need her, when I've never needed anyone before.

And right now, I need to get out of my own head. I refocus on Crystal. "I thought I sent you home long ago."

He head lifts and she shuts her computer. "I have your bags. I wasn't about to make your day worse by not having them." She shoves her notebook into her oversized purse that clearly doubles as a briefcase. I watch her delicate little hands, wondering why I don't mind when she touches me. And why I want her to touch me now.

She hikes her bag onto her shoulder, thrusting her chest out in the process, and my gaze drops to the high neckline of her dress, the material hugging her in all the right places as she walks toward me.

She stops in front of me. "How's your mother?"

"Putting on a show of bravery she doesn't feel."

With a grim nod, she agrees. "Yeah. I kind of got that, too."

For a few moments I just stare down at her, puzzled by this woman in too many ways to count. "You seem rather fond of my family, for someone who's only known them for three weeks."

"Actually," she corrects, "I met your mother at a Riptide auction I attended with my father and brother about a year ago. I'd been working at a small gallery a few blocks from Riptide and we sort of became friends." She smiles with a memory, and it's genuine in a way so few are. "When the sales manager's job came open, your mother all but tied me to the desk and insisted I take it."

I could think of a lot of places to tie this woman up, and none of them are to a desk, though that holds interesting potential. "I'm surprised it took her a year to hire you."

"I'm as stubborn as she is, and I thought we'd have issues working together. But it turns out we're a great team."

"Seems that way," I agree, having seen how fond my mother is of her. I motion to the exit. "Ready?"

She nods. "If you're ready, I'm ready."

My lips twitch. "That's the most agreeable you've been since I met you."

She grins. "Don't get used to it."

I pull the Mercedes up in front of my hotel, and I have no desire to be alone with my thoughts. "Come in," I tell Crystal. "I'll buy you dinner."

"That's not necessary."

"I don't remember saying, or thinking, it was," I reply. When her eyes meet mine, for some reason I know that she feels like an obligation and it bothers her. Why would she assume such a thing? Who has made her feel that way? Nudging her, I add, "I'm not looking forward to staring at a hotel room wall for the next few hours. Spare me that, please."

The valets open her door and mine. "You told your mother you're tired," she reminds me, then laughs. "And she seemed to think you look that way, too."

My brows lift. "That may be true. But it still doesn't mean I can sleep." It's an admission I normally wouldn't make. I seem to be doing a lot of things with this woman I wouldn't normally do, and I'm not sure if that's because of her or me.

She considers me a moment, then smiles. "Well, I *am* hungry."

"Good," I say, more pleased than I should be by the prospect of a simple shared dinner as we exit the car. But I really don't want to be alone with my thoughts, and my normal outlets to escape are back in San Francisco, in the club I own.

We head inside the typical high-end hotel of marble and glass, and I pause in the entryway to give the doorman a hefty tip. "Make sure my bag is in my room when I get there later tonight." He quickly nods, eager to oblige, and I turn to Crystal. "Let me check in so I don't have to deal with it later."

"Of course," she agrees, and she motions to a couple of chairs. "I'll be right here."

A few minutes later, I'm done registering and I find Crystal with her head buried in her laptop again, so absorbed in her work that she has no idea I've stopped in front of her.

"Ms. Smith," I say.

Her gaze lifts and snaps to mine. "Crystal, or I'm not having dinner with you."

My lips quirk, and I'm remarkably amused by her spunk. "What are you working on?"

"I'm this close," she says, holding her fingers up barely parted, "to snagging a couple of super-rare Beatles items for the next Riptide auction. I'm exchanging emails with the guy we'd be buying from."

"Beatles, huh?"

"Yes," she says, shutting her computer and shoving it into her purse. "It might not be art, but these items will bring in big money."

"You won't see me complaining about money," I assure her. "Shall we go eat?"

She pushes to her feet but I don't step back to give her space. We're toe to toe, and I can't seem to find a reason, aside from her being off-limits, to find this a problem. I'm in no hurry to move, either. Instead, I inhale that warm rum scent of hers. It is addictive. Damn, I like that smell.

"I'm ready," she says, prodding me to move. "Starving, actually."

Yes—starving. I'm starving. For her. So much so that I have to force myself to finally step back and give her room to walk. "Never let it be said I kept a starving woman waiting." I usually do keep my women starving and waiting, just not for food. I'm not so sure this one would allow that, though, which should be a complete turn-off. It isn't. It's more of a challenge.

"You like word games," Crystal observes.

I tilt my head slightly. "What did I say to merit that observation?"

"It's what you didn't say," she replies, "and yet it's in the air. That unspoken hidden meaning to a lot of what you say and do."

"You *are* direct, aren't you?"

"We've already established that. And that I'm hungry, so feed me. How about it?"

My lips twitch. "How about it, indeed." I motion her onward and this time we fall into step together. This dinner is absolutely going to be the much-needed distraction from the hell going on in my head—exactly what I'd hoped for.

A few minutes later, I'm seated across from Crystal inside the hotel-sponsored Fireside restaurant at a corner table. Seated behind the rectangular bar with snowball-shaped glowing lights dangling above it, we're secluded from the rest of the patrons, just as I'd hoped. I want this woman to myself, if only for an hour.

"Have you ever eaten here?" she asks, setting her phone on the table and her purse in the extra chair next to her. "The food is good. It's not far from the gallery I used to work at."

"I have," I tell her. "And yes, it is. How do you feel about wine?"

"I love it, but I'm a lightweight so it's not a good idea."

"Maybe it will loosen you up and you'll tell me all about yourself."

She snorts and somehow it's delicate and feminine, even sexy, when normally I would find it unrefined. "Do I really seem like I need loosening up? Because that's a first. I'm me, no matter what, and I make no apologies for that. And what specifically do you want to know that I haven't already told you?"

Everything, I think, but the waiter stops beside me before I can offer her my edited version of that answer. I glance at the wine menu and then at her. "Red wine okay?"

"I prefer white, but I have to drive, so I'd better pass."

Ignoring her objection, I order a merlot I'm particularly

fond of and send the waiter on his way. "I'll get you a car to take you home and pick you up in the morning."

She holds up her well-manicured hands. "You don't have to—"

"I don't do anything because I have to, Crystal."

"*Crystal*," she repeats. "Why do I feel it's such an accomplishment for you to use my first name?"

"I don't know? Why?"

Her brow furrows. "You really do like word games, don't you?"

"Do I?"

She holds up a finger. "See. Answering a question with a question. Word games." Her phone rings and she snatches it up and her eyes brighten. "It's my Beatles man. Calling rather than emailing has to mean good news."

I listen to the smooth, charming way she greets her customer and the impressive way she navigates her side of the exchange. She's a master of conversation, but I knew that already. I'm not beyond seeing how she's worked her magic on me.

The waiter returns with our wine and pours some into my glass for me to test the vintage when Crystal covers the phone and whispers, "He won't ship the items. He says we have to pick them up."

I sample the wine and give the waiter the go-ahead to fill both of our glasses. "Tell him we'll insure them."

"He axed that idea before I even got it out. He says it isn't good enough." She crinkles her nose. "He's a little eccentric."

Eccentric artists and collectors are my life. "Where's he located?"

"Los Angeles."

"If it's worth my time, I'll go pick up the items myself."

"Perfect." Her attention goes back to her call. "How about I arrange the pickup and call you tomorrow?" She listens a moment, and repeats what she said to me. "Yes. I'll talk to you then." Setting her phone back onto the table, she grins. "Done. We have a deal."

"I take it you feel the travel is worth my time?"

"I had the items valued by a Beatles expert. They're costing us a hundred thousand dollars." She lifts her wine and holds it out to me. "They're worth double."

"Impressive," I say, and touch my glass to hers. "Sounds like we need to feed his eccentric demands."

We both sip our wine.

"Hmm," she says. "This is excellent, but"—she sets her glass on the table—"I have to drive. I really can't drink."

"I've already told you I'd get you a car service."

"No, I—"

"I just bought the wine. I can't drink it alone."

"Yes, but Mark—"

"You're staying," I insist, and I'm amazed by how much I like my name on her lips, when I'm used to Mr. Compton or Master. I like it. I like it a hell of a lot.

She purses those too-tempting lips and then sighs. "Fine." She reaches for her glass. "But if you're hoping to find out some deep, dark secrets about me that somehow make me a bad employee, you won't. Not even with the grape in me." She takes a drink and casts me a coy look. "But I might try to find out yours."

"You can try. Others certainly have."

"But you've never had *me* try."

"No," I agree. "I've never had *you* try." And since I'm adamant about my privacy, why do I want her to try?

The waiter returns in the midst of my contemplation and we order dinner. When we're alone again, Crystal digs into the warm bread he's left us and I'm drawn to how uninhibited she is. Her lack of walls and barriers must be why I find myself so comfortable with her.

"A hamburger, Mr. Compton?" she queries. "How very rustic of you."

"I can get my hands dirty when I want to."

Her eyes twinkle devilishly. "I think I might like to see that."

There's a challenge beneath her words. For me to show her? I'd like to show her, but I won't. I almost think she knows that, and is enjoying taunting me. "And I'd like you to tell me more about you."

"Translation," she replies, and flattens her hands on the table. "You want me to convince you that I can handle my job when you're back in San Francisco and your mom is recovering." She sits up straighter, as if preparing to give a speech, and delicately clears her throat. "Mr. Compton. I'd like to submit to you my qualifications as sales manager for Riptide." She grins. "Beatles, baby. Doesn't that say it all?"

I tilt my head to study her. "Beatles, baby?"

"I guess that just broke all your rules times ten."

"Who says I have rules?"

She waves off my question. "Oh, please. You have so many

rules, your rules have rules. Any woman who dared to date you would need an encyclopedia-sized book to keep up."

"Any woman who *dared* date me?"

"Yes. You're too good-looking and rich for anyone's good. But I'm sure there are plenty of women who dare. They probably stand in line for a chance to read your rule book."

From anyone else, being called good-looking and rich would be a compliment. I'm not sure with Crystal. I'm not sure of too much with this woman.

"But not you," I say, certain that's what she meant. No. She wouldn't line up for anyone. She wouldn't be that easy to conquer.

"I'm a control freak," she readily admits. "You're a control freak. We'd be like two bulls after the same red scarf."

She's right, and yet my blood pumps faster, just thinking about having her naked and willingly at my mercy. I can't help but think she's exactly what I need: a challenge. And how sweet her submission would be, because I'd really earned it.

But I won't go there. Not with someone I work with, and absolutely not in the deep, dark hell I'm in right now. I'll just think about it. Probably way too much.

Four

—

Crystal tells me stories about my mother over dinner, making me laugh. I don't laugh a lot, but I have a soft spot for my mother. Maybe I have a soft spot for Crystal. I'm not really sure what I think about my reactions to her.

"So . . ." Crystal says, mopping up the last of her vanilla ice cream with a forkful of chocolate cake. "Why don't you work here in New York?"

I drum my fingers on the table. "And here I thought you'd used such great restraint, not prying into my secrets."

"So you admit you have secrets."

She's quick-witted. I like that about her. "We all have secrets."

"Some more than others."

I lean forward, lowering my voice. "And what are your secrets, Crystal?"

"They're called secrets because they're secrets," she replies tartly, to put me in my place.

I've done my damnedest to keep my thoughts pure over dinner, but my cock thickens with what I see as a challenge.

Can I make her reveal all to me? Instantly, I'm delving into the deep, dark waters of desire for this taboo woman, wondering what it would take to learn her secrets. Wondering how she would handle me tying her up. That's when you see what people are really made of.

"Back to you," she directs, as if she's in charge, when she absolutely is not. "And the question you avoided several times already. Why'd you leave New York?"

I lean back in my chair, putting distance between us and studying her, intrigued by how well she handles herself. It is both a natural gift and a conditioning of those skills by life lessons. I wonder what hers have been. "If I don't tell you why I left, my mother will, which is one answer to your question," I finally concede. "While my family is private about most things, they tend to make my life much more public than I prefer. Distance gives me privacy."

"That's not an answer." Her tone is a schoolteacher reprimand. "It's a side step of the question yet again."

She's right. I am sidestepping. My reasons for leaving New York run through a muddy history I try not to travel. I sure as hell don't talk about it.

My cell phone rings, giving me a reprieve, and I glance at the screen and see Chris Merit's number. It's a call I need to take, yet dread answering for many reasons. Not only is he involved with what went down with Rebecca, he's also deeply involved with a cancer research organization.

I hit the "answer" button, not bothering with "hello."

"I hear you're back in Paris."

"I am. How are you holding up?"

Uncomfortable with where this conversation is going, I glance at Crystal and cover the phone. "Give me just a minute."

"Of course," she says and reaches for her wine. "I'll just drink, since I handle it so well."

So far she's handled it just fine, I think, leaving the table so I can talk more privately. "I was going to call you," I tell Chris, leaning on the bar with my back to Crystal. "I'm in New York. My mother has cancer."

Silence ticks by for several heavy seconds. "What kind and what stage?"

"Breast. Stage 3."

"Operable or nonoperable?"

"Operable. She's having a mastectomy tomorrow and starts radiation in three weeks."

"That's positive," he says, and they're welcome words from a man who says little and is so knowledgeable about cancer. "You know, we've had our differences, Mark, but I'll walk through hell and back to help you help her, if you need me to."

"I know." The gnawing in my gut starts all over again, this time created by guilt. I knew Sara meant a lot to him, but I tried to get between them. She reminded me of Rebecca, and I was pissed at Chris for warning Rebecca away from me. He was right, though. Rebecca should have stayed the hell away from me.

"Mark. You still there?"

Mentally, I shake myself. "Yes. I'm here."

"You didn't cause Rebecca's death. You know that, right?"

The pain moves to my chest and becomes crushing. "I used one woman to keep another at a distance. One of those women killed the other one. How is that not my fault?"

"You didn't do this. Ava killed Rebecca."

My other hand curls into a fist on the bar. "I should have listened to you when you said Rebecca was in over her head with me."

"Don't do this to yourself. Take it from me—I've been down this path. I'm still on it now. It won't lead you anyplace good."

"You don't know everything. She left me for another man. She was traveling the world with him, living the good life, and I convinced her to come back to me. That things would be different between us. I don't know what the hell I was thinking. I knew I was incapable of being different. And she did. She came home, and Ava got to her before I could. I didn't even know she'd returned."

Silence stretches between us, and I am certain he's judging me—and, for once, I know it's deserved. Hell, *I'm* judging me.

"I know this is hard to swallow," he finally says. "I know it's eating you alive, but this was the work of one crazy woman. Not you."

"A woman I pushed over the edge."

"I could tell you everything you need to hear, but you won't hear me. Sometimes there's only one solution."

"And that would be?"

"Get drunk."

I laugh humorlessly. "This coming from a man who hates booze."

"There are times when it's called for. I could use a good stiff drink right now myself. What's going on with the investigation into Rebecca's death?"

While I fill Chris in, I turn to check on Crystal, and my

eyes collide with hers. I feel the connection with a surge of adrenaline like nothing I've ever experienced. No woman affects me like this. None. Ever. What is it about Crystal? Is it the challenge? The time in my life?

"I'll call you tomorrow to check on your mother," I hear Chris say.

"Right." I can't look away from Crystal. And "can't" isn't usually in my vocabulary. "Tomorrow. I'll talk to you then."

"She's going to be fine," Chris adds and hangs up, as if he wasn't ready to hear any other answer.

I'm not, either. She *has* to fucking be okay. There isn't another option, and damn it, I plan to tell her that in the morning.

Sliding my phone back into my pocket, I motion the waiter over and have him put the tab on my room and order a car to pick up Crystal. The distraction does nothing to stop the heat racing through my blood. I walk toward Crystal, fighting that predatory male instinct I own as completely as my name. That part of me that wants to take her upstairs and fuck her until I remember nothing but the pleasure. I need that. I need it like I do my next breath, but I know it's wrong. I know I've been so fucking wrong this past year about too much. I can't do it again. I won't do it again. I won't fuck up Crystal like I did Rebecca.

I stop in front of Crystal's chair and, unable to resist the need to touch her, when I'd swear I never need to touch anyone, I hold out my hand and she slides her palm into mine. It's tiny and soft, as I know she would be in my arms. I pull her to her feet, so close that the delicious scent of her is licking at my senses the way I'd like to be licking at her mouth, her body.

Her gaze lifts to mine, and there is heat in those intelligent blue eyes—but there's also concern that tells me she sees far more than she should. Far more than I let anyone see, and yet I still hold on to her hand. She's real to me in a way no one else has felt in too long. In a world that seems painted in false shadows, I need something real in my life right now.

"Everything okay?" she asks softly.

"No. Everything is not okay." I have no idea why I've admitted this. What the fuck is this woman doing to me? I'm feeling angry. I want to bury myself in her and forget everything, and it kills me to know how wrong that is. How impossible.

Her expression softens. "I know, and I'd tell you it's going to be okay—but that won't make it better and it won't make you believe it."

Almost exactly what Chris said, and he understands me because he's like me. Maybe she is, too. Truly, though, I have no clue. I've never been so clueless. I need to get away from this woman before I make another mistake we'll both regret. I release her hand and step back from her. "I'll walk you to the car I just had ordered for you."

"You don't have—"

"I'm walking you to the car."

"Okay." Her chin lifts with challenge. "You have my permission to walk me to the car."

My lips tighten and so does my groin. "As long as I have your permission," I say sardonically.

She simply gives me a nod and starts walking and, as I'm becoming accustomed to, she seems to expect me to follow. And holy hell, I do. But I want to grab her and pull her to the elevator and upstairs, where I can punish her with pleasure for making me this willing to chase her.

Once we're outside, and a driver opens the door to the black sedan I've hired as her ride home, Crystal turns to me. Her mood has softened. "I'm going to the hospital in the morning, and I have to pick up my car here. You want to ride with me?" Her eyes light with mischief. "I'll let you drive."

That's it. I grab her and pull her to me. "You'll let me?"

She blinks up at me, and I watch the emotions flicker over her face, from stunned to aroused, and then to rousing challenge. "If you ask nicely," she assures me, and no matter how coolly she tries to deliver the words, she can't hide the breathless quality to her voice.

"I wonder if you'd ask nicely?" I'm not talking about driving the car, and I know she knows it.

Her lips curve into a teasing smile and she pushes out of my arms, stepping closer to the car. "I wonder." She slides into the backseat and the driver shuts the door behind her.

I don't move, staring at the tinted window, certain she is staring back at me, looking for a reaction I won't give her. The car pulls away from the curb and, with adrenaline licking at my limbs all over again, I turn away and head into the hotel. Alone. I am alone. It has never mattered before. It's always been my preference, but tonight . . . tonight I hate it.

Once I'm in my room, the first thing I do is call my father to check on my mother. She's sleeping and my father sounds like utter shit. He's exhausted and worried, and for the first time in a long time I don't know how to make things right. I pace the room, the booze I'd tried to drown this with having absolutely no effect. Chris's advice sucked. I go to my suitcase and open it. On top is a red leather journal and a small velvet box. I take them both to the bed and set them there.

I stare at the two items and finally manage to open the box to stare at the rose-shaped ring nestled in the black velvet. The one Rebecca had worn when she'd been my submissive. I want to flush it down the toilet, as much as I want to cherish it forever. It is a part of her, but it's also the symbol of what led to her destruction . . . our bond.

I sit down on the bed, open the journal, and start to read. I know it's not a good idea, but I can't seem to help myself. And damn if I don't hear Rebecca's voice in my head. *He is my Master, the one who commands me, but he is so much more to me. Am I foolish to believe I am more than a sub to him? Am I insane to believe that deep beneath his hard surface he might have real feelings for me?* I've memorized this passage and heard it as if she were reading it to me a million times over. I've read it often since finding one of her journals under the mattress of my bed months ago, when she'd left town with another man. My bed. I cringe. I'd always made her feel everything had been mine, not hers, even when she'd lived with me. It is one of the many things I regret about the past that I can now never mend. She deserved better than me. She deserved the love I couldn't give her, yet I selfishly called her back to San Francisco, knowing I could never be all she wanted me to be. She would never have been attacked had I not done such a thing. I'd been the end of her. Never again will I pull someone into the BDSM world who's not already there and reveling in the experience.

My thoughts go to Crystal, and my new resolve forms. I won't touch her.

It simply can't happen. I won't let it.

No matter how much I want her.

And I do.

Five

—

*B*etween my guilt over Rebecca and my worry over my mother's surgery, sleep is nearly impossible. Knowing I'm not likely to leave the hospital today, I dress in boots, jeans, and a brown Riptide T-shirt. Remembering the colder East Coast weather, I slip on a brown leather jacket.

Crystal is waiting for me in the lobby when I step off the elevator. Dressed in dark blue jeans, a pale blue silk blouse, boots, and a black leather jacket, with two coffee cups in her hands, it's clear she doesn't plan to head to Riptide today, which pleases me. Though I should want her there at Riptide, taking care of business.

She gives my similar attire an open inspection and smiles. "I like you like this," she says. "Less 'master,' more man." I stiffen at the "master" reference, and my eyes narrow, trying to read her. Does she know more about me than I think she does? And, holy hell, do my parents? She thrusts the cup at me. "White mocha."

I reach for the coffee, unsure of what she knows. I am on

such unsure footing with this woman, I barely know myself. "White mocha?" I inquire, never having had anyone assume this to be my drink. But then, people don't get the chance to assume with me.

She nods and sips from her drink. "My favorite, and all macho alpha men like you have a secret softer side and a sweet tooth. It's part of the breed."

She's dead-on. I have a major sweet tooth, but I don't admit it. "Macho alpha men?"

She pushes her tousled blond hair out of her face. "Alpha man. Control freak. Type A personality, which I share. Whatever you want to call it, it's you. Anyway, try the drink. The place I got it from is a block away and open twenty-hour hours. It's really pretty good."

Already my resolve to keep a distance from her is crumbling. Her outrageously bold personality seems to work for me. "Considering the time change and the early hour, I can certainly use the caffeine. Thank you."

"My pleasure," she says, holding up her keys for me.

I take them from her, thinking her pleasure is exactly what I'd like to discover. Once we're in the car, she keeps me talking and I let her. Anything to keep my own thoughts at bay.

*T*hirty minutes later, I stand by my mother's bedside and lean down to her. "You're going to be okay."

She grabs the back of my head and pulls me close. "Yes," she vows. "I will." She hugs me so tightly, I feel like she's clinging to me for dear life.

My eyes burn and my chest is on fire. She releases me and I lift my head to find Crystal standing in the doorway. There's no hiding how emotional I feel, and I don't even try. This woman is seeing parts of me I show no one. Parts I'm not sure I believed existed anymore, and I'm beyond stopping her. She's too present. Too deeply embedded in my family's life. This is why I need to be in San Francisco. It's why I left.

The doctor enters and sends us on our way, so I give my mother another kiss, leaving my father alone with her. Out in the hallway I walk to the waiting room and sit down, letting my head drop into my hands, elbows on my knees.

I feel Crystal next to me. And then her hands are in my hair, she is touching me, and I don't push her away. There is tenderness and comfort in her touch, comfort I swear I don't need . . . and yet I do.

Slowly, I lift my head and look at her, staring into those pure, blue eyes, and feel like my heart's being ripped from my chest. I feel something for this woman. I swore I'd never feel anything for anyone again, and for ten years I've managed to hold to that vow. Now, though . . . I am lost and she has found me.

"Three hours," she whispers. "It seems like forever, but it'll be fast. She'll be out of surgery and feisty as ever, telling you how things are, and ruling the world."

I laugh humorlessly. "Please let that woman make my life hell for another hundred years."

Crystal smiles. "Don't you worry. She'll outlive us both." She reaches into her purse and grabs a deck of cards. Then she moves a small table and sets it in front of me before pulling a chair up opposite. "Let's play. What's your game?"

This is another part of my past I don't want revealed, and I'm suddenly aware of how exposed I am with this woman. Too exposed. "I don't play cards."

"Oh, come on. You're human. You play cards."

"No, Ms. Smith. I do not."

"Crystal," she corrects softly, "and if that's true, then there's no better day to learn. It'll occupy your mind, which I happen to know is too sharp to remain inactive for the next three hours."

"I'd rather discuss the auction coming up."

"Poker? Why, yes, I'd love to play."

I glance up to find my father, and it's impossible to miss how bloodshot his eyes are. He grabs a chair and pulls it between mine and Crystal's. He lifts his Styrofoam coffee cup. "Nothing better than coffee and poker, except beer and baseball." He glances at Crystal. "Look out, darlin'. Mark was a damn good player back in his college days. He was the undefeated champion. If not for—"

"Dad," I warn, stopping him and then looking at Crystal. "Deal."

She studies me a moment. "Whatever you want, Mr. Compton."

And damn if I don't correct her. "Mark. My name is Mark."

Three hours later I've won every hand of poker, and my father and Crystal are laughing as they team up against me and threaten to count cards.

"That's only done in Blackjack," I remind my father.

"Mr. Compton?" a man says.

We all rise and turn toward the doctor who's standing in his scrubs, his mask on his chest, looking calm. Every muscle in my body eases. "She's doing well," he reports, and my shoulders slump, the tension sliding from my weary body, as he adds, "You can see her soon."

I glance down at Crystal, who smiles at me. And for the first time in days, I truly breathe again.

I'm still talking to the doctor when Crystal gets a call. By the time the doctor departs, she's grabbing her purse and walking toward me. "I need to run over to Riptide. Can you please tell your mother I was here and I'll be back as soon as can?"

"Is there a problem?"

"Nothing I can't handle."

"What's wrong, Crystal?"

She surprises me by reaching out and pressing her hand to my chest. "Trust me, please. Go be with your mother. I won't let you, or your parents, down."

Heat radiates from the place she touches, and yet I'm frozen in place. "I don't trust easily."

Her fingers curl on my chest. "I suspect you don't trust ever."

"And yet you're asking me to trust you."

She wets her lips and I want to lick them, too. "You get nothing you want if you don't ask for it."

The air pulses around us and my hand closes over hers. "You have no idea how much I agree."

"So you'll go be with your family and let me take care of business?"

"Yes. I will."

"Mark," my father says, and I release her hand.

Six

—

A few hours later, the hospital phone in my mother's room rings. She shifts against her pillow, still stubborn enough to try to answer it, and moans with the pain that creates.

"Oh, no, you don't," my father says, quickly moving from his chair to her bedside, while I swipe the phone from the table.

"Compton room," I answer.

"Mark?"

At the sound of Crystal's voice, I glance at the clock, and note that it's four o'clock. "I thought you were coming back."

"I am. I sat in a traffic jam for over an hour, and once I got here there were all kinds of things the staff needed for our small Monday event that I didn't plan on. You know how it is around here."

"Is that Crystal?" my mother whispers hoarsely. "I want to talk to her."

"My mother wants to talk to you, but don't hang up until I speak to you again." I don't wait for her agreement—I assume it, as she does for far too many things—handing the phone over to my father.

I watch as he holds it to my mother's ear so she doesn't have to lift her arm, and the tenderness of his expression rips through me. My parents' relationship is not all roses. They've made each other's lives hell. I know this, though no one else does, and it's made me doubt what people so flippantly call "love."

Until now. Until this moment, when my mother is broken, and my father is by her side, and I see this look on his face. I see that, despite all they have been through, a part of him would die if we lost her.

My father removes the phone from my mother's ear and I reach for it a moment too late. He hangs it up.

I wait for it to ring again. And wait. Crystal doesn't call back. I *told* her I wanted to talk to her. I run my hand through my hair and walk to the window. It's all I can do not to call her back and demand an update on Riptide's affairs. I can't and won't try to run two operations in separate states, worrying about what I don't know when I should. If she wants my trust, she needs to communicate with me.

*B*y the time visiting hours end, Crystal hasn't called or shown up. I'm reclining in a green chair, much like the one my father has folded out into a bed, while my mother sleeps deeply, tucked beneath her sheets. Though I have Crystal's cell number, I don't use it. The more time goes by, the longer her silence draws out, the more I want to call her—but not here, not when it might upset my mother.

I uncurl myself from the chair and walk to my mother's side, kissing her forehead. She doesn't move, and neither does my father. Reluctantly, I head out of the room, caving to my father's request that I give them some alone time in the evenings, which I know is a ploy to get me to rest.

Once I'm in the hallway, I dial the security desk at Riptide and confirm everyone is gone for the weekend, including Crystal. Irritated, I head to the front of the hospital and hail a cab to take me to my hotel, contemplating my next move. I decide I want to see *her* next move instead. Will she show up at the hospital tomorrow, or go silent on me? If she goes silent, she's a problem I need to know about now, not later.

Fifteen minutes later, my cab stops at the hotel and I head up to my room. There I strip and go straight to the shower. I've tossed on pajama bottoms and I'm towel-drying my hair when a knock sounds on the door. Tossing the towel into the sink, I walk to the door, expecting the maid service. "I'm good. I don't need anything," I call out.

"It's me. Crystal."

I freeze. Crystal is at my hotel door? This is temptation and danger waiting to happen. This is . . .

I open the door. She's holding a folder in her hand, her purse over her shoulder. Her gaze slides over my naked torso and lifts, and I don't miss how hard she swallows. "You weren't answering your phone. I guessed you were in the shower and your dad gave me your room number, so I—"

I pull her inside and shut the door, and touching her is fire in my veins. A dark, familiar need inside me begins to demand satisfaction. That part of me that uses sex for escape, for control of everything in my life.

But she is not for me, and I am not for her. She knows this. I know she knows this. She shouldn't be here.

I quickly maneuver her against the wall and my hands settle by her head, my body lifting from hers. "Why are you here?"

"I have a situation I—"

"Why didn't you call me and check in today?"

"You needed to focus on your family."

"I told you I wanted to talk to you."

"And I avoided you."

"At least you're honest. Why?"

"Because I had a problem I was trying to solve, and I knew if I talked to you, you'd know about it."

"You don't think I needed to know there was a problem?"

"After it was solved, if I could solve it. And I did—one of them. There's another I need your help with."

"What are the problems?"

"One of the artists showing in Monday's mini-auction tried to pull out. It's handled."

"And the other problem?"

"My Beatles guy wants this done this weekend. I made reservations to fly out in the morning. I need you to sign the check and paperwork. Your father says he's not authorized, but you are."

I'm not even going to comment on why my father doesn't have access to the money. A piece of dirty laundry I didn't ever want revealed but she's managed to tread over. This woman keeps getting all up in my business. She keeps getting in my head. "You sure this has to happen now?"

"He's adamant."

My gaze finds its way to her mouth, and my blood runs hot. I want this woman. I want her, and I have her alone in my hotel room. "And you thought it was a good idea to come to my room to solve this?"

"Actually," she says, her voice hoarse, "I thought it was a very bad idea."

"And yet you still did it." It's not a question.

"I leave at six in the morning. I had no choice."

If I stay this close to her, I'm going to strip her naked and fuck her. I push off the wall and stare at her. "Show me the paperwork."

"I'll get it ready for you." She doesn't wait for my approval—she never does—but walks past me toward the desk. Her scent stays with me, lingering in my nostrils and thickening my cock. Her hips sway with feminine grace and I picture her on top of me, riding me.

I have two choices here. They are simple. I fuck her, or I don't. It doesn't get any more black-and-white than that. Everything changes in the morning, though. That's when everything gets complicated.

She pulls a folder from her purse and opens it. I walk over to her and stop beside her, just shy of our shoulders touching. She hands me a pen, and I take it without looking at her—and I damn sure don't touch her. Touching her would be bad. I sign the purchase order and then look at the hundred-thousand-dollar check.

Now I look at her, and her mouth is mere inches away—an easy lean in to meet her lips with mine. The burn to kiss her is intense. I don't kiss women. I fuck them. I please them. I like to please them. To drive them to the edge and make them want and want, until release is sweet bliss. But I don't kiss them.

I tap the pen on the check. "This is what I call trust." I sign the check and drop the pen, turning to face her. "Make sure you deserve it."

She lifts her chin. "You're insured if I don't, but you wouldn't have signed it if you didn't believe I was worth the risk."

There's a subtle challenge in her voice. There's a less subtle challenge in her eyes, a message. I grab her and turn her backside to the desk, my hips framing hers, my fingers wrapping her slender waist. "What did you think would happen between us if you came here tonight?"

Her hands settle on my arms. "I thought we'd end up naked."

I wonder if her directness will ever fail to surprise me, as much as I wonder what it is about her that gets to me. "And you don't see the problem in that?"

"I see a million problems with that. Do I care? At his very moment, with you half naked already, I can't seem to, no."

And neither can I. Therein lies the problem, but I can't stop myself from touching her, caressing a path up her sides and skimming the lush curves of her breasts. That I can't stop myself is a red flag, a sign I am not myself, and that I have no business doing this. But I watch Crystal's lashes flutter and her lips, those damn lips I want to taste, part. To possess this woman is like a drug I have to have. And I do have to have her.

Desire overcomes me, and it's a welcome replacement for what I've felt these past few days. Without conscious thought, I lace my fingers into the silky strands of her hair, and my mouth closes down on hers. The taste of her explodes on my tongue— addictive, sweet, with a hint of coffee. Her hands are all over me, her touch feeding the hunger in me, and I don't know why I don't stop her. Or maybe I do. Control means thinking, and thinking is more dangerous than this woman. Thinking is making me crazy, it's making me doubt, it's making me question all that I am or ever have been.

My hands hug her backside and I pull her hard against my thick erection. She moans, a seductive, wanton sound, and I am instantly harder, hotter. I am lost in her, in kissing her, in touching her, and I can feel how lost she is, too. I want her like I've never wanted anyone. She answers an invisible something inside me, and I don't know why or how.

She shrugs out of her jacket and I keep kissing her, hungering for more of her and ready to have her naked, to feel her soft skin next to mine. To bury myself in her and have her wet heat wrapped about my cock, taking me away to some oblivion that will never last long enough. My hands work her shirt up from her sides, my fingers finding her bra and shoving down the lace to tug at her nipples. She makes a tormented sound, tears her mouth from mine, and our eyes collide.

And holy hell—I don't know why, but the impact punches me in the chest again. For a moment we're frozen, looking at each other, and I'm not sure what I feel. It's unfamiliar, like everything this woman does to me. And the very fact that I crave more of it tells me I'm in trouble. I don't have control. She has it.

Crystal moves first, tugging her shirt over her head, and the broken connection of our stare is just enough to shake some clarity back into my mind. I step back and sit on the bed to watch her undress. I study every inch of her with a penetrating boldness that would make most women nervous. Not Crystal. She watches me watch her—desire, even challenge, in the depths of her stare as she unhooks her bra, as if she's telling me she knows what I'm trying to do. She knows I'm trying to rattle her, and it won't work.

Just when I'm about to order her to caress her breasts, her hands close around them, shoving them together, her thumbs moving over her nipples. My cock pulses at the sight of her, all wanton and eager to please. Or maybe she doesn't want to please me. Maybe she wants to control me with her body. It is not a pleasing thought. She's everything I don't like in a woman, and yet I can't take my eyes off her.

My gaze strokes over her body, watching her take off the remainder of her clothes. I'm not even attracted to blondes, usually. Yet every inch of her—from her pale hair to her pale skin, to the pale neatly trimmed V of her body—arouses me and spawns a million fantasies of what I could to do her if I had more than one night.

In some far part of my mind, I grapple to be myself, to take charge. I need to control this woman before she does what no other woman has, and truly controls me.

As if she wants to prove she can do that and more, she drops to her knees in front of me, her hands sliding up my thighs. "I've thought about"—she runs her teeth over her bottom lip—"what it would be like to make you—"

I don't let her finish the sentence. Warning bells go off in my head. She's just a few licks from taking me where I don't want to go. To have me at her mercy, not the other way around. I have her on her feet, backed against the desk again, before she knows what's happened. I press her hands to the desk. "Don't move them until I say you can move them."

Her lips curve into a smile. "You can fuck me, Mark, but you don't get to control me."

"We'll see about that," I say, and this time I drop to my knees, sliding my fingers over the slick center of her body.

She gazes down at me. "What does that prove?" she challenges, sounding breathless.

I slip a finger inside her. "You tell me."

Her lashes lower, then lift. "That you can make me feel good."

I press another finger inside her and stroke her. "And does that feel good?"

"Oh, yes," she whispers. "That feels good."

"And if I lick you? Will that feel good?"

Her thighs tense as if in anticipation. "Why don't you try it and see?"

I can't get this woman to back down. I'm going to *make* her back down. I run my tongue over her clit several times and then suckle her. Her hands go to my head and I shove them back on the desk. "Touch me and I'll stop."

"I'm going to touch you, Mark. If you don't like it, you picked the wrong girl to bury your troubles in."

I pull my fingers from inside her.

She groans. "That was rude."

"*That* was necessary," I assure her. My hands go to her hips and I stand up, lifting her to the desk at the same time. I move to step away from her, and she wraps her arms around my neck, pressing her breasts against my bare chest.

"Why can't you just fuck me?" Her hand slides to the top of my pajama bottoms. "Why can't you forget all the games just for one night?"

"There's no such thing as just fucking," I say, but it doesn't stop my mouth from closing over hers, and damn if she doesn't take that as an invitation. She all but climbs on me, wrapping her legs around me and lifting herself off the desk.

Her body molds to mine, her fingers delicately framing my face as she pants into my mouth, "You *can* just fuck me. Tomorrow you're still my boss."

I stand there holding her, telling myself she's wrong—but suddenly, I just don't care anymore. I don't care about anything but being inside her. Not who has control, not how this will end badly. There's only the need to be inside her. To "just" fuck her.

I set her back on the desk, one hand under her backside, and I'm not sure if she or I pull my shaft from the pajama bottoms, but I'm already thick between her thighs.

"Wait," she pleads urgently, and reaches into her purse, digging frantically until she pulls out a condom.

I stiffen, but it doesn't stop her from tearing the condom open. "My brother stuffed it in my purse a few weekends ago. He said I needed to get lucky."

It's all I need to hear. Already reality is sliding back into my mind, and I don't want it there. I snatch the condom from her, roll it over me, and press inside her. The warm heat of her body surrounds me, and I sink deep into her sex, groaning as she tightens around me, taking all of me.

"Just fuck me," she whispers against my ear.

Pulling back, I look at her, and heat expands between us, combustible, explosive. Suddenly, I'm kissing her again—or she is kissing me. I don't know which, but I've lifted her from the desk and I'm holding her against me and I barely remember doing it. I pump into her and she clings to me, making sexy little sounds that make me want to fuck her even harder, deeper. I can't get enough.

Turning her, I lay her on the bed and press her back into the mattress, lifting her legs over my shoulders. In some sane part of my mind, it's a safer position. She's more at a distance. She's *just* a fuck. But damn it, now she's looking at me, and every time I drive into her, I see her pleasure, and I see more. I see this woman who is more than just a fuck, and it's making me insane. And hot. And then even hotter. I can't thrust hard enough or get deep enough.

"Harder," she pants. "Harder."

I give her harder. I give her deeper.

"More," she demands. "More."

I have never had a woman demand anything from me. They beg. They plead. They call out "Master," as I command they do. But right now I would kill to have her say my real name. To plead for more from me. The *real me* I show no one.

But she doesn't. She moans loudly and stiffens, her sex closing down on me in a tight clamp a moment before the spasms overtake her and me. Damn it, I'm going to come. I don't want to come; I don't want to return to reality.

But I do. I come. There's a tugging sensation in my balls, and then I shake with the fierceness of my release. The world goes dark for a moment that's both eternal and too short.

Somehow her legs are no longer over my shoulders and my weight is on my elbows, my head buried in her hair. And her delicate little fingers are caressing the back of my neck. I don't want to move.

Then my cell phone rings, and the reality I've tried to escape slams into me like a concrete block. I jerk my head up, instantly worried that something is wrong with my mother. By the third ring, I've pulled out of Crystal, rounded the bed, and answered my phone. "Is everything okay?"

"It's fine, son," my father assures me. "I just wanted to be sure Crystal got hold of you."

I can hear her in the background, grabbing her clothes. "Yes," I say. "She got hold of me."

"She seemed fretful. What was going on?"

"She's flying out in the morning to make a large purchase."

"Tomorrow? Your mother will be upset she won't be here."

"The customer wouldn't have it any other way. How is Mom?"

"She's awake and in pain and asking for chocolate. She says it cures all. I don't want to leave her. Can you—"

"If you can get me past the nurses, I'll bring her some." A door opens and shuts, and I jerk around to find Crystal out of sight. "Let me call you back, Dad."

I walk to the bathroom to find it empty. Then a note pops under the front door, and I bend and pick it up.

Mr. Compton:

I'm sparing you the awkward morning after. This never happened. Okay, maybe it did. But this really was "just" a fuck.

Ms. Smith

Was it just a fuck? I'm not so sure. With Crystal, I'd lost the steely control I pride myself on, despite my guilt over Rebecca and my worry over my mother's surgery.

No. What happened tonight wasn't just sex. It was something else. Something very dangerous. Something I *will* *never* let happen again.

Can't get enough of
Lisa Renee Jones?

Start from the beginning with the first book in the
Inside Out series

If I Were You

On sale now!

One

Dangerous.

For months I've had dreams and nightmares about how perfectly he personifies the word. Sleep-laden, alternate realities where I can vividly smell his musky male scent, feel his hard body against mine. Taste the sweet and sensuous flavor of him—like milk chocolate with its silky demand that I indulge in one more bite. And another. So good I'd forgotten there's a price for overindulgence. And there is a price. There is always a price. I was reminded of this life lesson on Saturday night. And I know now, no matter what he says, no matter what he does, I cannot—will not—see him again.

It started out as any other erotic adventure with him. Unpredictable. Exciting. I barely remember where it all went wrong. How it took such a dark turn.

He'd ordered me to undress and sit on the mattress, against the headboard, my legs spread wide for his viewing. Naked before him, open to him, I was vulnerable and quivering with need. Never in my life had I taken orders from a man; most certainly I had never thought I would quiver with anything. But I did for him.

If Saturday night proved anything, it was that once I was

with him, under his spell, he could demand anything of me, and I'd comply. He could push me to the edge, to unbelievable places I'd never thought I would go. Exactly why I can't see him again. He makes me feel possessed, and what is so disconcerting about this feeling is that I like it. I can hardly wrap my mind around allowing such a thing, though I burn for it. But when I saw him standing at the end of the bed Saturday night, all broad and thick with sinewy muscle, his cock jutting forward, there was nothing but that need.

He was magnificent. Really, truly the most gorgeous man I've ever known. Instant lust exploded inside me. I wanted to feel him close to me, to feel him touch me. To touch him. But I know now not to touch him without his permission. And I know not to beg him to let me.

I've learned my lesson from past encounters. He enjoys the vulnerability of a plea far too much. Enjoys withholding his pleasures until I am nearly quaking with the burn of my body. Until I am liquid heat and tears. He likes that power over me. He likes full control. I should hate him. Sometimes, I think I love him.

It was the blindfold that should have warned me I was headed toward a place of no return. Thinking back, I believe it did. He tossed it on the bed, a dare, and instantly a shiver chased a path up and down my spine. The idea of not being able to see what was happening to me should have aroused me—it did arouse me. But for reasons I didn't understand at the time, it also frightened me. I was scared and I hesitated.

This did not please him. He told me so, in that deep, rich, baritone voice that makes me quiver uncontrollably. The need to please him had been so compelling. I put on the blindfold.

I was rewarded by the shift of the mattress. He was coming to me. Soon I knew I would come, too. His hands slid possessively up my calves, over my thighs. And damn him, stopped just before my place of need.

What came next was a shadowy whirlwind of sensation. He pulled me to my back, flat against the mattress. I knew satisfaction was seconds away. Soon he would enter me. Soon I would have what I needed. But to my distress, he moved away.

It was then that I was sure I'd heard the click of a lock. It jolted me to a sitting position, and I called out his name, fearful he was leaving. Certain that I'd done something wrong. Then relieved when his hand flattened on my stomach. I'd imagined the sound of the lock. I must have. But I couldn't shake the subtle shift in the air then, the raw lust and menace consuming the room that didn't feel like him. It was a thought easily forgotten when he settled heavy between my thighs, his strong hands lifting my arms over my head, his breath warm on my neck—his body heavy, perfect.

Somehow, a silk tie wrapped around my wrists and my arms were tied to the bed frame. It never occurred to me that he could not have done this on his own. That he was on top of me, unable to manipulate my arms. But then, he was manipulating my body, my mind, and I was his willing victim.

He lifted his body from mine, and I whimpered, unable to reach for him. Again silence. And the whisk of fabric. More strange sounds. Long seconds ticked by, and I remember the chill that snaked across my skin. The feeling of dread that had balled in my stomach.

And then, the moment I know I will die remembering. The moment when the steel of a blade touched my lips. The moment that he promised there was pleasure in pain. The moment when *the blade traveled along my skin with the proof he would be true to his words. And I knew then that I had been wrong. He was not dangerous. Nor was he chocolate. He was lethal, a drug, and I feared . . .*

A knock on my apartment door jolts me from the seductive words of the journal I've been reading to the point I darn near toss the notebook over my shoulder. Guiltily, I slam it shut and set it back on the simple oak coffee table where it had been left by my neighbor and close friend Ella Ferguson the night before. I hadn't meant to read it. It was just . . . there. On my table. Absently, I'd opened it, and I'd been so shocked at what I found that I hadn't believed it could really be my sweet, close friend Ella's writing. So I'd kept reading. I couldn't stop read- ing, and I don't know why. It makes no sense. I, Sara McMillan, am a high school teacher, and I do not invade people's privacy, nor do I enjoy this kind of reading. I'm still telling myself that as I reach the door, but I can't ignore the burn low in my belly.

I pause before greeting my visitor and rest my hands on my cheeks, certain they're flaming red, hoping whoever is here will just go away. I promise myself if they do, I won't read the journal again, but deep down, I know the temptation will be strong. Good Lord, I feel like Ella seemed to feel when living out the scene in the journal—like I am the one hanging on for one more titillating moment and then another. Clearly, twenty-eight-year-old women are not supposed to go eighteen months without sex. The worst part is that I've invaded the privacy of someone I care about.

Another knock sounds, and I concede that, nope, my visitor is not going away. Inwardly, I shake myself and tug at the hem of the simple light blue dress I still wear from today's final tenth-grade English class of the summer. I inhale and open the door to have a cool blast of San Francisco's year-round chilly night air tease the loose strands of my long brunette hair that have fallen from the twist at my nape. Thankfully, it also cools my feverishly hot skin. What is wrong with me? How has a journal affected me this intensely?

Without awaiting an invitation, Ella rushes past me in a whiff of vanilla-scented perfume and red bouncing curls.

"There it is," Ella says, snatching up her journal from the coffee table. "I thought I'd left it here when I came by last night."

I shut the door, certain my cheeks are flaming again with the knowledge that I now know more about Ella's sex life than I should. I still don't know what made me open that journal, what made me keep reading. What makes me, even now, want to read more.

"I hadn't noticed," I say, wishing I could pull back the lie the instant it's issued. I don't like lies. I've known my share of people who've told them, and I know how damaging they can be. I really don't like how easily this one slipped from my lips. This is Ella, after all, who in the past year as my neighbor has become my confidante, the younger sister I'd never had. Together we are the family neither of us has or, rather, neither of us wishes to claim. Uncomfortably, I ramble onward, a bad habit brought out by nerves, and guilt, apparently. "Long day of classes," I add, "and I had piles and piles of paperwork to finish up for the summer. Lucky you got to avoid that this year, though I had some great kids I enjoyed." I purse my lips and tell myself I've said enough, only to find I can't help but continue. "I only just got home a few minutes ago."

"Well, thank goodness you have some time off now," Ella says, lifting the journal. "I brought this over last night when we'd planned to watch that chick flick together. I wanted to read you a few of the entries. But then David called, and you know how that went." Her lips tilted downward, guilt laden in her tone. "I deserted you like a very bad friend."

David being her hot doctor boyfriend. What David wanted from Ella, he got. Now, I know just how true that is. I study Ella a moment. With her dewy youthful skin, and dressed in faded jeans and a purple tee, she looks like one of my students rather than a twenty-five-year-old teacher herself. "I was tired anyway," I assure her, but I'm worried she's over her head with this man ten years her senior. "I needed to get to bed to be ready for today's classes."

"Well, they're over now and yay for that." She indicates the journal. "And I'm so glad to get this back before my date with David tonight." She wiggles an eyebrow. "Foreplay. David is going to love this. This thing is scorching hot."

I gape in utter disbelief. "You read him your journal?" I'd never have the courage to read a man such intimate personal thoughts—especially not about him. "And it's foreplay?"

Ella frowns. "This isn't my journal. Remember? I told you last night. It's from the storage units I bought at that auction at the beginning of summer."

"Oh," I say, though I don't remember Ella saying anything about the journal. In fact, had she, I'm 100 percent sure I'd remember. "That's right. The storage auctions you've been attending since you got obsessed with that *Storage Wars* show. I still can't believe people store their things and then default and let it go to the highest bidder."

"And yet they do," Ella says. "And I'm not obsessed."

I arch a brow.

"Okay, maybe I am," she concedes, "but I'm going to make more than double what I would have teaching summer school. You should really consider going to the next auction with me. I've already turned around two of the three units I bought for big money." She holds up the journal. "This came from the last unit I bought, and it's the best yet. It has artwork I know is going to sell for big bucks. And so far I've found three journals that are absolutely spellbinding. My gosh, I can't seem to stop reading them. This woman started out like you and me, and somehow got pulled into this dark passionate place that is terrifyingly exciting."

She's right, and I can feel that burn in my belly as I recall the words on those pages. I can almost imagine the soft, seductive voice of the woman whispering her story to me. I try to focus on what Ella is saying, but I'm wondering about that woman instead, wondering where she is, who she is.

"Oh my!" Ella exclaims. "You're blushing. You read the journal, didn't you?"

I blanch. "What? I . . ." Suddenly, I can't talk. I am so not myself right now, and I sink helplessly into an overstuffed brown chair across from Ella, stuck in the trap of my earlier lie. "I . . . yes. I read it."

Ella claims a couch cushion, narrowing her green eyes on me. "Did you think I wrote that stuff?"

I cast her a tentative look. "Well . . ."

"Whoa," she says, clearly taking my reply, or rather lack of reply, as confirmation. "You thought . . ." She shakes her head. "I'm speechless. You couldn't have read the good parts or there's no way you would think she was me. But you're sure blushing like you read the good parts."

"I read some parts that were, ah, pretty detailed."

She snorts. "And you assumed I wrote them." She shakes her head again. "And here I thought you knew me. But heck, I so wish I could live up to that assessment for just one hot night. There is a mysterious eroticism to that woman's life that's just . . ." She shivers. "Haunting. It, she, affects me."

In some small way it comforts me to know she is as affected by the words on those pages as I am, and I don't know why. What in the world do I need comfort for? It isn't logical. Nothing about my reaction to this unknown woman is logical.

"Once David and I finish with the journal," Ella continues, drawing me back into the conversation, "he's going to take pictures of a few intimate pages for potential buyers and we're listing the journals on eBay. They're going to bring in big money. I just know it."

I gape, appalled at this idea. "You can't seriously intend on selling this woman's personal thoughts on eBay?"

"Heck yeah, I do," she says. "Making money is the name of the game. Besides, for all we know, it's fiction."

Her words are cold, and she surprises me. This is not the Ella I know. "We are talking about a woman's private thoughts, Ella. Surely, you don't want to profit off her pain."

Her brows dip. "What pain? It sounds like all pleasure to me."

"She lost everything she owns at auction. That isn't pleasure."

"I'm guessing her rich man flew her off to some exotic location and she is living life in a grand way." Her voice turns somber. "I have to think like that to do this, Sara. Please don't make me feel guilty. This is money I need, and if I didn't do this, some other buyer would have."

I open my mouth to argue but relent. Ella is alone in this world, with no family aside from an alcoholic father who doesn't know his own name most of the time, let alone hers. I know she feels she has to have money for emergencies. I know that feeling myself all too well. I, too, am alone. Mostly, but I don't want to think about that right now.

"I'm sorry," I tell her, and I mean it. "I know this is good for you. I'm happy it's working out."

Her lips curve slightly, and she nods her acceptance before she pushes to her feet. I stand with her and give her a hug. She smiles, her mood transforming into the instant sunshine I so often find she brings into my life. I love Ella. I really do.

"David and I are looking forward to a bit of that spellbinding action ourselves tonight," she announces mischievously. "I have to run." She laughs and waves a few fingers at me. "Enjoy your night. I know I will."

I sink back into my chair and watch the door close.

*T*he sound of pounding on my door once again takes me from bliss to panic. I sit up in the bed, disoriented and groggy, and eye the clock. Seven in the morning on my first day off from classes.

"Who the heck is pounding on my door?" I grumble, throwing the blankets off me and sliding my feet into the pink fuzzy slippers one of my students gave me last Christmas. I grab my long pink robe that is not fuzzy, but does say PINK across the back. More knocking has begun.

"Sara, it's me, Ella!" I hear as I shuffle my way toward the living room. "Hurry! Hurry!"

My heart flutters not only because Ella is clearly in some sort of panic but also because, unlike me, who doesn't like to waste a second of any day, Ella doesn't get up before noon on days she doesn't have to. The instant I yank open the door, Ella flings her arms around me and announces, "I'm eloping!"

"Eloping?!" I gasp, pulling back and tugging Ella inside, out of the chill of the early morning. She's still wearing her clothes from the night before. "What are you talking about? What's happening?"

"David proposed last night," she exclaims excitedly. "I can hardly believe it. We're flying to Paris this morning." She eyes her watch and squeals. "In two hours."

She shoves something into my hand. "That has the key to my apartment. On the kitchen table, you'll find the journal and the key to the storage unit. If it's not cleared out in two weeks, it has to be rented, or it's auctioned off yet again. So take it and sell the stuff. The money is yours. Or let it go. Either way, it doesn't matter." She grins. "Because I'm eloping to Paris, then honeymooning in Italy!"

Protectiveness fills me for Ella. I don't want her to get hurt, and I've never even heard her say she loves David. "You've known this man for only three months, sweetie. I've met him only once." He always, conveniently, got called away when we'd been planning to get together.

"I love him, Sara," she says, as if reading my mind. "And he's good to me. You know that."

No, I don't know that, but while I try to find the right way to say it, she is already reaching for the door. "Ella—"

"I'll call you when I arrive in Paris, so keep your cell handy."

"Wait!" I say, shackling her arm. "How long will you be gone?"

Her eyes light up with excitement. "A month. Can you believe it? A whole month in Italy. I'm living a dream." She hugs me and gives me a kiss on the cheek. "Since we high school folks don't go back until October, thanks to the longer school days, I'm going a full month! Can you believe it? I'll never complain about our longer school days again. A whole month in Italy—I'm living a dream! I'll call, and when we get back we'll have a reception."

Her eyes soften. "You know I wanted you with me for this, don't you? But David knew I had no family. He wanted to whisk me away so that it wouldn't be painful." She pokes at the puckered spot that always appears between my brows when I frown. "Stop making that face. It'll be wrinkled when you get older. And I'm fine. I'm perfect, in fact."

"You better be," I say, attempting my best teacher voice, but my throat is too tight to do much more than croak out the warning. "Call me as soon as you arrive so I know you're safe, and I want pictures. Lots of pictures."

Ella smiles brightly, "Yes, Ms. McMillan." She turns and rushes away, giving me a last-second wave over her shoulder before she rounds the corner. She is gone, and I am fighting unexpected tears I don't even understand.

I am happy for Ella but worried for her, too. I feel . . . I'm not sure what I feel. Lost, maybe. My fingers curl around her keys, and I am suddenly aware that I have just inherited a storage unit and the journals I swore I wouldn't read again.